MADE FOR HER

What Reviewers Say About Carsen Taite's Work

Trial and Error

"Everything I love in Carsen Taite's books is in this one: the law, the flawed characters, the excitement of the plot."—*Jude in the Stars*

"Another good installment in *A Courting Danger Romance* series. I love when writers bring their expertise in a subject matter into their novels. Carsen Taite is one of them, as a retired criminal defence attorney, her legal thrillers are unique in our genre."—*Lezreviewbooks.com*

Trial by Fire

"My favourite Carsen Taite books are the ones in which her background as a criminal defense lawyer shows. This one falls into that category. Everything about the MCs' jobs was exciting, the inner workings of the courthouse, the atmosphere, the differences between the PD office and Wren's high profile law firm but also the differences between the PD office and the DA office. The way the philosophies clash yet both offices need the other, two sides of the Justice coin. Taite's insider knowledge shows in tiny details, and I would happily have read more about cases and untangling facts and lies to reach as much of the truth as possible."—*Jude in the Stars*

Her Consigliere

"With this sexy lesbian romance take on the mobster genre, Taite brings savvy, confidence, and glamour to the forefront without leaning into violence. ...Taite's protagonists ooze competence and boldness, with strong female secondary characters. ...This is sure to please."—*Publishers Weekly*

"...a very enjoyable thriller/romance with intrigue, well-developed characters, and a beautiful love story. I had a lot of fun reading this book, and would love to see more of these characters."—*Rainbow Reflections*

Spirit of the Law

"I would definitely recommend this to romance fans and those that like their romance to include lawyers and a little bit of mystery. Due to the slight paranormal elements I think paranormal romance fans would also enjoy this even if they don't normally read Taite."—*LGBTQ Reader*

Best Practice

"I think this could very well be my favourite book in this series. *Best Practice* is a light and easy opposites-attract age-gap read. It's well-paced and fun, not overly angsty, with just enough tension to be exciting."—*Jude in the Stars*

Drawn

"*Drawn* by Carsen Taite is a compelling mystery and romantic suspense novel that will keep you glued to your couch or wherever the reading frenzy catches you. …This novel is so much more than a mystery and romance because it deals with family relationships, heartbreaking internal struggles and emotional baggage that many people have to deal with. There's no doubt about it, Carsen Taite definitely deserves the highest of fives for bringing this story to life for me!"—*The Lesbian Review*

Out of Practice

"Taite combines legal and relationship drama to create this realistic and deeply enjoyable lesbian romance. …The reliably engaging Taite neatly balances romance and red-hot passion with a plausible legal story line, well-drawn characters, and pitch-perfect pacing that culminates in the requisite heartfelt happily-ever-after."—*Publishers Weekly*

Still Not Over You

"*Still Not Over You* is a wonderful second-chance romance anthology that makes you believe in love again. And you would certainly be missing out if you have not read *My Forever Girl* because it truly is everything."—*SymRoute*

Leading the Witness

"Carsen Taite is a sure bet."—*Jude in the Stars*

Practice Makes Perfect

"Absolutely brilliant! …I was hooked reading this story. It was intense, thrilling in that way legal matters get to the nitty gritty and instill tension between parties, fast paced, and laced with angst. …Very slow burn romance, which not only excites me but makes me get so lost in the story."—*LESBIreviewed*

"…a fun start to a promising new series, with characters I enjoyed getting to know."—*Lesbian Review*

Pursuit of Happiness

"Taite has written a book that draws you in. It had us hooked from the first paragraph to the last. We thoroughly enjoyed this book and would unhesitatingly recommend it."—*Best Lesfic Reviews*

"…an entertaining read for anyone interested in American politics and its legal system."—*Lez Review Books*

Love's Verdict

"Well written, cleverly plotted, with a great balance between the slow change from dislike to attraction to love in the romance department while the high profile case works through its phases. The merging of the two plots is subtle and well-crafted seamlessly moving us forward on both fronts. The high profile murder is well played, as always with Ms. Taite's courtroom dramas, and I liked the way it became a real life thriller as well as a legal case. Overall an excellent read, one of my favourites from this author."—*Lesbian Reading Room*

Outside the Law

"This is by far the best book of the series and Ms. Taite has saved the best for last. Each book features a romance and the main characters, Tanner Cohen and Sydney Braswell are well rounded, lovable and their chemistry is sizzling. …The book found the perfect balance between romance and thriller with a surprising twist at the end. Very entertaining read. Overall, a very good end of this series. Recommended for both romance and thriller fans. 4.5 stars."—*Lez Review Books*

A More Perfect Union

"Readers looking for a mix of intrigue and romance set against a political backdrop will want to pick up Taite's latest novel."—*RT Book Reviews*

"…an excellent romantic suspense (which should be a surprise to no one, because that's exactly what Taite does!). …This is a pitch-perfect Carsen Taite story. Everything worked for me!"—*Lesbian Review*

Sidebar

"Sidebar is a love story with a refreshing twist. It's a mystery and a bit of a thriller, with an ethical dilemma and some subterfuge thrown in for good measure. The combination gives us a fast-paced read, which includes courtroom and personal drama, an appealing love story, and a more than satisfying ending."—*Lambda Literary Review*

Letter of the Law

"If you like romantic suspense novels, stories that involve the law, or anything to do with ranching, you're not going to want to miss this one."—*Lesbian Review*

Without Justice

"Another pretty awesome lesbian mystery thriller by Carsen Taite."—Danielle Kimerer, Librarian, Nevins Memorial Library (MA)

"All in all a fantastic novel...Unequivocally 5 Stars..."—*Les Rêveur*

Above the Law

"...readers who enjoyed the first installment will find this a worthy second act."—*Publishers Weekly*

Reasonable Doubt

"The two main characters are well written and I was into them from the first minute they appeared. It's a modern thriller which takes place in the world right now."—*Lesfic Tumblr*

Lay Down the Law

"Recognized for the pithy realism of her characters and settings drawn from a Texas legal milieu, Taite pays homage to the prime-time soap opera *Dallas* in pairing a cartel-busting U.S. attorney, Peyton Davis, with a charity-minded oil heiress, Lily Gantry."—*Publishers Weekly*

Courtship

"This is one really fine story. I felt as if I were right in the middle of a major political battle to get a relatively unknown woman appointed to the most important court position in the land. Levels upon levels plus twists and turns, including a passionate entanglement adding a spectacular underscore, as the lovers meld and re-meld multiple times. I would have to say this is a classic page-turner and I totally enjoyed the high-spirited elements that may always surround key political battles. Magnificent!"—*Rainbow Book Reviews*

Switchblade

"Dallas's intrepid female bounty hunter, Luca Bennett, is back in another adventure. Fantastic! Between her many friends and lovers, her interesting family, her fly by the seat of her pants lifestyle, and a whole host of detractors there is rarely a dull moment."—*Rainbow Book Reviews*

Rush

"A simply beautiful interplay of police procedural magic, murder, FBI presence, misguided protective cover-ups, and a superheated love affair...a Gold Star from me and major encouragement for all readers to dive right in and consume this story with gusto!"—*Rainbow Book Reviews*

Battle Axe

"Taite breathes life into her characters with elemental finesse. ...A great read, told in the vein of a good old detective-type novel filled with criminal elements, thugs, and mobsters that will entertain and amuse."—*Lambda Literary*

Slingshot

"The mean streets of lesbian literature finally have the hard-boiled bounty hunter they deserve. It's a slingshot of a ride, bad guys and hot women rolled into one page turning package. I'm looking forward to Luca Bennett's next adventure." —J. M. Redmann, author of the Micky Knight mystery series

Nothing but the Truth

"As a criminal defense attorney in Dallas, Texas, Carsen Taite knows her way around the courthouse. ...*Nothing But the Truth* is an enjoyable mystery with some hot romance thrown in."—*Just About Write*

It Should be a Crime—Lammy Finalist

"This [*It Should be a Crime*] is just Taite's second novel..., but it's as if she has bookshelves full of bestsellers under her belt. In fact, she manages to make the courtroom more exciting than Judge Judy bursting into flames while delivering a verdict. Like this book, that's something we'd pay to see." —*Gay List Daily*

By the Author

Truelesbianlove.com

It Should be a Crime

Do Not Disturb

Nothing but the Truth

The Best Defense

Beyond Innocence

Rush

Courtship

Reasonable Doubt

Without Justice

Sidebar

A More Perfect Union

Love's Verdict

Pursuit of Happiness

Leading the Witness

Drawn

Double Jeopardy (novella in Still Not Over You)

Spirit of the Law

Her Consigliere

Perilous Obsession

Made for Her

The Luca Bennett Mystery Series:
Slingshot
Battle Axe
Switchblade
Bow and Arrow (novella in Girls with Guns)

Lone Star Law Series:
Lay Down the Law
Above the Law
Letter of the Law
Outside the Law

Legal Affairs Romances:
Practice Makes Perfect
Out of Practice
Best Practice

Courting Danger Romances:
Trial by Fire
Trial and Error

MADE FOR HER

by

Carsen Taite

2023

MADE FOR HER

ISBN 13: 978-1-63679-265-1

This Trade Paperback Original Is Published By
Bold Strokes Books, Inc.
P.O. Box 249
Valley Falls, NY 12185

First Edition: March 2023

CREDITS
Editor: Cindy Cresap
Production Design: Susan Ramundo
Cover Design By Tammy Seidick

Acknowledgments

I think one of the reasons I'm so attracted to books about the mob is the concept of a chosen family. Setting aside the violence and the defiant breaking of the law, these cohorts in crime pledge their undying allegiance to their self-selected families and I can totally relate to the concept. *Molte grazie* to my sister in crime, Ali Vali, a dear friend, who shared one of her most treasured characters with me for *Her Consigliere* and this story.

Thanks to everyone at Bold Strokes Books for giving my stories a home and treating them with such care. Special thanks to my smart, funny, and very patient editor, Cindy Cresap, who I'm lucky to call friend. Tammy, thank you for another fantastic cover.

Writing is fifty percent putting words on paper and fifty percent thinking about, planning for, and talking about putting words on paper—tasks made easier with the help of good friends, and I have the good fortune to have a lot of those. Hugs to Georgia, Melissa, Kris, Elle, and Ruth. Special thanks to Paula for being my ride or die—there's never been a better pal.

Thanks to my wife, Lainey, for always believing in my dreams. This year has been a wild ride full of change and I love our new adventures.

And most importantly, many thanks to you for reading my work. Whether you're a first time Carsen Taite reader or a loyal supporter who's read my work for years, I'm forever grateful for your support. Every story is for you.

Dedication

To Lainey. We are definitely made for each other.

CHAPTER ONE

It sucks to be the tall one in a gunfight. The thought whizzed through Neal's mind as she ducked to avoid the bullets pounding the wall behind her. She hunched behind the staircase railing, slammed a new clip into her weapon, and glanced over to her right where Don Mancuso's bodyguard, Michael, was defending his former boss's office door with his huge, broad body which had already taken a hit. They needed reinforcements and they needed them fast.

Keeping her eyes trained on the landing, she reached for her phone and speed-dialed Robert Valentino, one of the Mancuso capos who was supposed to have followed them upstairs. The minute the line connected, she whispered, "Get everyone to the front of the house. Take no prisoners." She hung up before Robert could question her logic or authority since she didn't feel like explaining the former and she wasn't sure about the latter. Don Mancuso had been in the ground less than a week before his enemies had begun this assault, and with his consigliere, Siobhan Collins, having fled the country within hours of his death, none of the foot soldiers left behind was certain who was in charge. Their enemies were taking advantage.

She crawled toward Michael and motioned for him to get down. As she drew closer, she pointed to the door behind him. He nodded and fired another round toward the first floor before joining her as she dove into the Don's private office.

"Grab everything from the desk," she whispered, as she surveyed their options for escape. "The key's in there. Book of Acts," she added, pointing to the worn King James Bible sitting on the surface. Siobhan had alluded to the hiding spot on her most recent call, saying the only way to salvation was through the verses urging action. She hoped she hadn't misread the clue.

"Got it," Michael said, holding up the key in triumph before using it to open the Don's desk. A moment later, his arms stuffed with papers, he stood and inclined his head toward the door. "They'll be here any minute. You have a plan?"

She should. There'd been plenty of opportunities to practice the skills she'd learned over the years as a loyal soldier and protector of the Don's consigliere, but nothing truly prepared a person for their world to come crumbling down upon them. She had only her instincts to trust. "Let's draw them in."

Michael didn't hesitate. He picked up a chair and hurled it at the closed office door, instantly drawing fire. If the men downstairs weren't already on the landing, they would be running toward them now, determined to gun them down. She pointed to the window and ran toward it, throwing open the sash to look out onto the balcony. The drop to the ground was about thirty feet. Survivable, but likely crippling. Even with her natural agility she wasn't likely to survive a fall like that and Michael would hit the ground like the boulder he was. She glanced up at the roofline, a mere shoulder pull from the balcony railing away.

"Come on," she yelled to Michael, no longer trying to hide. The intruders knew they were in here and in a minute, they'd be right where she wanted them.

Michael frowned but followed her command and joined her on the balcony. "No way, I'm going to survive," he said, looking downward.

"True. That's why we're going this way," she said, pointing at the roofline. She stepped onto the railing and clambered onto the roof. Once she was settled, she reached down a hand. "You got this."

His eyes were wide, but he tucked in and climbed onto the railing while she prayed it would hold him. It took both of them, but they managed to get him up and onto the roof after a few stressful tries.

"What now?" he asked.

She pointed down. "Get ready to shoot."

As if on cue, two heads appeared below them. She could only imagine their thoughts as they looked at the lush lawn below, wondering why there wasn't any sign of the bodies that had plummeted there to escape them.

"They're gone."

"Because you're slow. It took you a year to climb the stairs. They can't be far on foot. Let's go find them."

Neal heard the thick burr of the Russian accents, instantly knowing who'd sent them. If she would only wait, they would leave the house to continue their pursuit, but the trouble with guys like these was they would come back, again and again, until their work was done. She held her gun, trained between them both for the few seconds it took for her to reach a conclusion. *Pop. Pop.* From a distance, the shots probably sounded more like a toy than the real thing, but the blood that fanned out on the chest of each man told a different story. Seconds later, two more men appeared, but this time Michael took aim and took them out.

"You think there's more?" she asked Michael.

"Not today."

He was right to make the distinction. This was only the first delegation. The Mancusos had plenty of enemies. What she needed right now was to figure out who their friends were. "We need to get out of here."

"We can go to the lake house."

Neal nodded, but her mind was processing all the angles. The Don's house on the shore of Lake Ray Hubbard was a palatial getaway. When he'd escaped to the oasis in the past, a full contingent of bodyguards accompanied him. But since his death and Siobhan leaving the country and his other daughter, Dominique's betrayal of the family, the family had been fractured and she wasn't confident there were enough loyal foot soldiers to adequately guard the mansion on the lake. What she needed more than a retreat was some ammo to use on offense. "You go. I want to do some checking around. I'll be at Siobhan's apartment. The feds have already tossed it and they aren't likely to be back soon."

"The feds aren't the only ones we need to worry about. Take some of the guys with you."

Again, he was right, and she nodded her assent, but she'd already decided she was going alone, certain a contingent of armed men riding up the elevator to the penthouse suite of Siobhan's fancy building would only draw unwanted attention.

In all the time she'd guarded her boss, she'd taken pains to be subtle—a feat made hard enough by her own towering frame. She might not know exactly who was behind the assault on the Mancuso family holdings, but she knew it was going to take some careful maneuvers to get answers.

Thirty minutes later, she pulled the Range Rover she used to drive Siobhan around town into the parking garage at the building and took the elevator to the top floor. She'd entered Siobhan's place on her own on dozens of occasions, but never under these circumstances, and the eerie quiet of the empty apartment echoed fears she'd been stuffing since Siobhan had fled the country with the federal agent who'd been assigned to investigate her. As she walked through the apartment, she replayed her last conversation with Siobhan.

"You're in charge for now," Siobhan said. "You've been in the room for enough strategy sessions to know what to do."

"I have one job—protect you. That's kind of difficult to do when you slip out of the country without telling me where you're going. You're with her, aren't you?" Neal shook her head, angry that she sounded like a jealous lover instead of the bodyguard who'd lost her protectee. She took a deep breath and tried again. "Royal Scott is a federal agent. Do you honestly think she can shrug off her instincts so easily?"

Siobhan's voice was silky and smooth. "Nothing worth having comes easy. When this is all over, we will have all given up a lot." She cleared her throat and when she spoke again, her voice was commanding, like she was standing in the well of a courtroom, making her case before a jury. "With his dying words, Don Carlo placed me in charge. If you don't trust me, then you doubt him."

There was no question, no specific ultimatum, but Siobhan's message was clear: to question her decisions was to test her loyalty, and there would be only one winner of any such test. "Understood. What would you like me to do?"

Siobhan had directed her to contact an old friend, telling her she'd find the number in Don Carlo's office, which was why she and Michael had been there this afternoon. She totally got why Siobhan didn't want to give her the information on the phone, but getting shot at hadn't been the ideal situation for hunting around in Don Carlo's papers. She'd wound up gathering everything from the drawer Siobhan had directed her to, and now that she was settled, she set the contents on the table to comb through them. Before she got started, she poured two fingers of Siobhan's expensive whiskey into a glass and inhaled the aroma before taking a long sip. The burn took the edge off the day and relaxed the muscles in her back which had been twitching since she'd bent herself into a pretzel to avoid getting shot.

Most of the papers were invoices for various businesses owned by the family, but tucked in with them was a plain-looking business card for a law firm in Louisiana. Muriel Casey. The last name was familiar and not just for obvious reasons. Muriel had been one of the last calls Siobhan had made before she and Royal fled the country. Neal flicked the card between her fingers for a few minutes, and then picked up her cell and punched in the numbers.

"Law firm," the voice on the other end of the phone was crisp and business-like.

"Muriel, please."

A few beats of silence passed before the voice on the other end of the phone asked, "Who's calling?"

Now it was Neal's turn to pause. Muriel wasn't likely to remember her name, but dropping Siobhan's over an unsecured line wasn't good strategy. She ran through several options in her mind before settling on one. "Please tell her another lawyer referred me to her. She would've handled my case herself, but she's traveling for an indefinite period of time."

"Hold please."

Neal sat through the cloying hold music, hoping Muriel's friendship with Siobhan extended to taking calls from strangers who needed way more help than a bit of legal advice. A few minutes later, her hopes were rewarded when a brisk, no-nonsense voice came on the line.

"I understand you need a lawyer."

Neal grunted. "That would be a good start."

"My secretary can schedule an appointment for you."

"I was hoping to talk to you now."

"I don't do phone consultations."

"Okay." Neal waited, unsure of what to say next, and willing Muriel to chime in with a solution. She was the lawyer, after all. For the most powerful crime family in New Orleans. She didn't have the time or interest to help Neal. "Is there any way you could make an exception?"

"I have an appointment in a few minutes. My secretary stepped out for about five minutes. If you call back then, she can schedule you an appointment. Please give her a couple of different numbers where you can be reached."

Neal heard the unspoken message, and the minute Muriel clicked off the line, she went to Siobhan's bedroom. She'd watched her boss place and remove valuables from the large safe in the wall behind her lavish wardrobe on many occasions, and she hoped Siobhan hadn't removed all of the supplies from the go-bag she hadn't had a chance to take when she'd left a week ago.

She needn't have worried. There were several disposable cell phones, still in their packaging along with a stack of fake IDs and several bundles of hundred-dollar bills. She tore through the packaging for one of the cell phones. She still had a couple of minutes to spare before calling Muriel back, so she dug a little deeper in the wall safe and came up with several handguns. Siobhan hated having them here and professed she'd never use them, but she'd been trained to use a firearm from the time she was a teenager. Neal checked the clip on the Ruger before shoving it in her waistband. She left the other two, one for Siobhan and one for Royal, so they'd have weapons when they came back since customs frowned on folks bringing their own.

If they came back.

It was the first time she'd allowed herself to think the unthinkable. She'd spent most of her adult life in the employment of the Mancuso family. Could this really be the end of the empire, and if it was, what was she supposed to do next?

She sat on the edge of Siobhan's bed and caught her breath. One step at a time. Call Muriel. Make a plan. Execute the plan. She dialed the phone and waited through the rings, forcing anxious thoughts away. When Muriel finally answered, she expelled a breath and gripped the phone.

"Neal?"

"Yes."

"I understand you need a legal consultation."

Neal heard the circumspection in Muriel's voice and took the signal she should do the same. "I do."

"I can represent you, but I want to make sure no one else is on the line with you, because if we're speaking privately, anything you say to me is privileged."

Neal held out the phone and stared at the screen. Muriel's message was loud and clear. She thought someone might be listening in, and if it was law enforcement, they wouldn't be able to use anything they said if it was spoken in the context of a client sharing information with her lawyer. She couldn't promise the apartment wasn't bugged—she hadn't had a chance to check it since Siobhan left, and there wasn't really any need to once she was gone. But even if it was bugged, it was too late now. "I'm alone."

"That's good. Tell me the nature of your question."

She had a lot of questions, but most of them started with what the fuck and ended with what the hell do we do now, neither of which was productive. She took a few seconds to distill her thoughts and blurted out: "I don't know where she is, but I need to talk to her. We need to know who's in charge."

A few beats of silence passed and Neal started to wonder if the call was still connected when Muriel cleared her throat. "You can't talk to her."

"Why not? Why can't I use this phone and give her a shout?"

"Neal, you need to understand what I'm saying."

She did and she didn't. This cagey dance was getting to be a little extra. "I need you to say something I can actually understand," she growled. "How about that?"

"She said you had a bit of a temper. That it might be your tragic flaw."

"The world's on fire and you think I have an anger management problem?"

"Focus. You don't need me to tell you who's in charge."

Neal chafed at the admonition. She was plenty focused. She'd been focused on survival since the moment Don Carlo died and her boss skipped town with her new girlfriend who just happened to be an FBI agent. Her entire world was not only on fire, it was upside down and she had no idea who she could trust. She knew Siobhan trusted Muriel Casey, but she didn't know her other than the fact she was the cousin of the infamous Cain Casey, and she owed Cain the same debt she owed Siobhan and the Mancuso family. She closed her eyes and took a deep breath like she used to do right before tip-off, centering herself for the battle on the court. Except this time there were no rules, or referees, or buzzers to signal the end of the game. Because it wasn't a game. The battle was real, and the stakes were higher than a championship ring.

She summoned all the strength she could muster. "Tell me what to do."

"Siobhan trusts you to do what's right."

Again, with the vague, non-answers. Neal resisted the urge to slam down the phone. "What's right is not as easy to figure out right now. Care to be a little more specific?"

"I don't have to be. You've been at Siobhan's side for years now, and she was at the side of your Don. Succession is a powerful force."

Neal bit down on her lip to keep from voicing her reaction. The line of succession in the Mancuso family was definitely not straight, but no way was she part of it. Right? Or maybe her job was to serve as a placeholder until Siobhan returned. If that's what she needed to do to ensure Siobhan's role was secure when she returned, she could do that. She would do that. "Fine. I'm in."

Muriel's laugh was hard. "That's right. You'll be just fine."

"You really don't know when she's coming back?" Neal asked, hopeful that because she'd agreed to serve as backup for Siobhan she might be entitled to a little bit more information.

"I have to go," Muriel said. "Don't use this phone again."

She punctuated her point by disconnecting the line, leaving Neal standing in the middle of Siobhan's apartment with more questions than answers. She wanted to put her head in her hands and surrender to her powerlessness, but she knew the moment she embraced her surrender, the more likely it was she wouldn't survive it. She wouldn't use the cell phone again, but now she had names and a place to search. It was time for her to take control.

Chapter Two

Anastasia Petrov flinched at the crash of the downstairs door and the subsequent creaks as it shuddered on its hinges, and she gave thanks again she'd insisted on the heavy oak with the metal. Her reasoning at the time had been protection from the outside, but she knew without looking the source of the banging was closer to home.

She rose from her chair and checked her reflection in the mirror. She'd dressed for an elegant dinner, taking special care with her hair, her makeup, and clothes to give the impression of success and fortune. To the casual observer, she'd pull off the charade, but she spotted the tiny wrinkles starting to form around her eyes and the tired stretch of skin along her neck. She'd shed the glow of youth without ever having had time to indulge in its glory. People referred to her as regal, grand— and she took great care to reinforce the image by dressing perfectly, painstakingly conscious of her appearance, but the days of allure were over and the best she could hope for now was grand dame, a role she'd embraced without affection.

She walked to the railing of the grand staircase, the centerpiece of this home, and called out to the man responsible for all the noise. "Mikhail, what did that poor door ever do to you for you to treat it so?"

His laugh was loud and raucous, signaling his mood. "Why are you still in your robe? Tonight is for celebration. Get dressed and meet me downstairs. Come quickly."

She didn't have to ask the source of his exuberance. Only one thing would put him in such a good mood—the fall of the house of Mancuso, and though she doubted it was as easy or foregone as he seemed to think, humoring him had become second nature. It was easier and, more importantly, it was safer.

She waited until he'd left the room before summoning Katia, her best friend and trusted assistant. Katia answered her text with a simple "*be right there*" and she showed up less than a minute later from her room in the other wing of the massive palace Mikhail had insisted on building when they'd moved to the States.

"What's going on?" Katia asked. "I heard Mikhail come in and he sounded excited."

Ana brushed her hair as she spoke. "I don't know this for a fact, but I believe he's finally conquered the Mancusos. I certainly don't know of anything else that would get him so excited."

"You underestimate yourself. As usual."

Ana considered the familiar refrain. Katia had never been afraid to voice her opinion, and she'd always been quick to state she was too good for Mikhail. Her blistering honesty was one of the reasons she'd insisted Katia immigrate with them as a condition of her agreement to marry him. She needed at least one ally here in the states because the size of Mikhail's ego crowded everything else out, and her own happiness was no exception.

"You know there's no longer anything there. If there ever was."

Katia sank into the chair next to her vanity and crossed her arms over her chest. "You don't have to stay, you know."

She made it sound so easy. Like there were a host of options available to her, but the truth was much more complicated. She was a Russian woman, living in the US on a visa procured by her father, a powerful figure in her homeland, but unlikely to have much sway here anymore since public opinion toward anything and anyone Russian had taken a sharp downward turn following the invasion of Ukraine. Her visa was intricately linked to her husband's legitimate shipping business which only served as a cover for their family's extensive underground criminal enterprises. If she were to leave, she would call unnecessary attention to all of it and there would be a steep price to pay.

"My time will come, but it is not now. I have work to do here, but in the meantime, I've been informed that tonight we're celebrating. Please come with us." She reached for Katia's hand and squeezed it tightly. "I would like a friend with me tonight."

"Of course." Katia stood. "Whatever you need. You know I will always be here for you. I'll get dressed and meet you downstairs."

Ana watched the door close behind her as she left, wishing she had the freedom to come and go as she chose, but choice was not a concept she'd had the opportunity to embrace. Still, she was not without power. She finished dressing and walked down the hall to Mikhail's suite, pausing only briefly to knock on the door before pushing her way in.

He was seated in front of a mirror, and she pictured him falling into the glass so closely was he examining his own face. He spotted her reflection, but didn't turn around. "You couldn't wait to see me, yes?"

"I came to tell you that I invited Katia to join us this evening."

"That's not what I had in mind."

"What did you have in mind, Mikhail? I'm weary of trying to read your thoughts."

He turned in his seat and shot her a piercing look. "You barely even try. You are my wife, and I do not wish for extra company tonight. Tell her she is not welcome."

"But she is. And I may be your wife, but you would do well to remember that all of this," she gestured at the opulent furnishings, "is possible because of my family's money. You work hard, but you are only building on a foundation that was laid for you. Do not forget the debt you owe." She delivered the words with bravado, but she knew she was stepping very close to the line they'd both respected as a means to keep up appearances. "Surely you would not deny me the company of a dear friend when we have such a big occasion to celebrate?" she asked to soften the blow of her declaration.

He calmed a bit at the last words—his shoulders relaxed and his scowl softened. He raised his hands in surrender. "Yes, of course. Bring her. Bring anyone. It is indeed a night to celebrate."

As long as he could pretend an idea was his own, there was peace in the house. But was peace worth the sacrifice?

She shook away the thought because to pursue it meant following a path that would only lead to trouble, and she'd spent her entire life avoiding conflict. She had money and status, and nothing had ever seemed worth the strife of fighting what would likely be a losing battle and nothing probably ever would.

An hour later, the limo dropped them off at Mikhail's favorite steakhouse. She and Katia followed Mikhail and his hulking flank of bodyguards inside where they were immediately led to a private lounge. Bottles of Cristal jostled in buckets of melting ice, and Mikhail wasted no time popping the cork and drinking straight from one of the bottles. He held it out to her, his glinting eyes challenging her to accept the dare. She offered him a smug smile while she cringed on the inside and took the bottle and tipped it toward her lips. The effervescent bubbles tickled her tongue, but she held the bottle in place several seconds longer than he had—a message to anyone watching that she was a power in her own right, worthy of running their business and deserving of respect. When she finally lowered the bottle and placed it back in the bucket of ice, Mikhail started a slow clap that grew in intensity.

"This is my wife," he proclaimed in a loud voice, silly due to the fact everyone there knew exactly who she was. "She can do anything I can do. But faster and smarter." The last words carried an edge that probably only she could hear, but there was no mistaking it was there. It accompanied the flash of temper in his eyes. Jealousy was a strong and dangerous emotion. She would do well to remember that.

"You flatter me, Mikhail." She pointed to the table and took a seat. "Tell us how you defeated the Mancusos." She asked the question to give him space to be the big man, but she genuinely wanted to know the answer. Less than two weeks ago, Don Mancuso's consigliere, Siobhan Collins, had sat in their living room trying to broker a truce. How had overtures of peace turned into seeds of war so quickly, and why hadn't she known what was happening?

He took another drink and wiped his lips with the back of his hand. "Brute force. That little bitch attorney fled the country after her boss died, and they left no one of substance behind."

"What about the daughter. Dominique? Isn't she still around?"

"She is. But she's been cast aside by her family." He raised his glass again in a lonely toast. "Thankfully, I was waiting in the wings to welcome her into our fold."

He leered then, and she tamped down the urge to back away, knowing he was performing for everyone else at the table. Neither of them were foolish enough to believe there would ever be any intimacy between them, but that didn't mean he could handle the reminder in public. Let him leer—it was the only satisfaction he would ever have.

An hour later, she watched while Mikhail flirted one last time with the waitress while he settled the check. The server tossed her hair and giggled a fake laugh, and Ana wondered if anything pierced the bubble of self-indulgence he'd enveloped himself in. Doubtful.

After he paid, Mikhail rose from the table and signaled to one of his guards before turning to her and Katia. "I have a meeting, but Sergei will see you both home," he said, referring to the head of his security.

Knowing that "meeting" likely meant a trip to one of the many brothels he liked to frequent, Ana saw a window of opportunity, and waved off his hulking escort. "It's still early, and I would like to do some shopping. Katia and I will be fine." She reached for her phone. "I'll call a car to take us."

He leaned in close and pecked her on the cheek. "You're so independent. What a charming trait," he said, the growl in his tone belying the words. He reached into his pocket and drew out a wad of cash. "Have a nice time, ladies." He tossed a stack of hundred-dollar bills on the table. "On me."

He turned to Sergei and snapped his fingers. So many ostentatious displays of faux power. It really was too much. When he finally disappeared, Ana pointed at Katia's drink. "You need to empty that right now. I'm ready to have some fun of my own."

Chapter Three

Neal stood at the end of the bar at Club Sanctuary, trying to act like her only care in the world was getting one of the busy bartenders to make her a drink, certain anyone watching could see through the ruse. When had she lost her ability to keep her cool?

When she'd stopped being someone else's bodyguard and had to focus on keeping herself alive.

She needed purpose, which was exactly the reason for her visit here tonight. Before Royal had burst into Siobhan's life and exploded it all to hell, Siobhan had spent a lot of time at this place, taking pleasure in the arms of strangers. Women she'd use to satisfy her urges in the rare moments when she wasn't fully focused on her work as Don Carlo's consigliere. Neal had witnessed the beginning of every such encounter, standing off to the side, taking great care to appear nonchalant while being hyper vigilant about protecting her charge.

Now Don Carlo was dead and Siobhan was gone and the Mancuso family empire was teetering on the brink of demise. For all she knew, everything she spent years dedicated to protecting was no longer relevant. What was she supposed to do now?

Find someone who might know where Siobhan was. Right. She took the cold glass of vodka and soda the bartender handed to her noticing the light brush of her fingers lingering a moment after the handoff was complete. She broke the contact by raising the glass to her lips, and she took a healthy swallow, enjoying the cool trickle of vodka and lime down the back of her throat.

"I've seen you here before," the bartender said, her lips curling into a sly smile. "But this is the first time I've seen you drink."

Neal raised the glass. "Cheers to the attentive bartender."

"Honey."

"Excuse me?" The touch was one thing, but the term of endearment was a bit much.

The bartender stuck out her hand. "My name is Honey. In the spirit of you loosening up, I figured we should be on a first-name basis."

This was the point of the encounter where the other woman expected you to reciprocate with some flirty banter or personal disclosure, but Neal wasn't up for either so she dodged. "Names are overrated. And who says I'm loosening up?"

"Mr. Tito says you are." She pointed at the glass in Neal's hand. "Ready for another?"

Neal looked down, surprised to see that barely a quarter-inch of vodka covered the bottom of the glass. She shouldn't have more—liquor was going to stall her search—but turning down the offer wasn't the way to get information. She nodded and handed her glass back across the bar. Honey took her time, dipping the ice into the glass, pouring the ice-cold vodka from a foot above the glass.

"You're pretty good at that."

"I'm good at a lot of things. Ditch your girlfriend and I'll show you."

"What makes you think I have a girlfriend?" The question spilled out before she could stop the words, but she was genuinely curious.

Honey made a show of looking around before leaning across the bar and whispering in Neal's ear. "The tall leggy brunette who looks like she eats fire for breakfast. The one who you stick to like glue. Where is she tonight?"

Good question. Neal focused more on the fact she'd like to know the answer than correcting Honey's misimpression of her relationship to Siobhan. She flashed back on her conversation with Muriel with renewed frustration about the lack of information. How was she supposed to defend the family's interests when the family had scattered to God knows where? Maybe she should get a clue and take off on her own.

She shook her head. She didn't even know what being on her own would look like. Except for her regular visits to the home where her sister lived, the Mancusos were the only family she'd known since she'd dropped out of Tulane years ago. Leaving when their situation was in chaos was tantamount to betrayal, and she wasn't a traitor.

She raised her glass and faked a smile. "Just me tonight. I was hoping maybe you'd seen my friend."

Honey laughed. "Friend, right." She used air quotes to emphasize her disbelief. "Not a sign of her tonight, but I haven't been here long. You want me to ask around?"

"No," Neal answered quickly. The last thing she needed was to fuel the rumors that Siobhan had taken off following the Don's death. She was as well suited as anyone else to find out where she was, and she could do it on the down low. She picked up her glass and eased away from the bar. "Thanks for the drink."

"I get off at two." Honey grinned. "Or I could if you want to stick around."

Neal grinned back but kept walking. While the prospect of sex with a stranger was alluring, Honey was a little too observant for a casual encounter. She'd have to find another way to take the edge off. In the meantime, she needed to focus. She glanced upstairs to the balcony. It would be the perfect place to look for any of Siobhan's prior trysts. She turned to head to the stairs and crashed into a woman rushing through the crowd. Vodka and soda soaked them both.

"Dammit." The woman stopped and wiped the front of her dress.

Neal started to reach out to help her but drew back her hand when she realized how much bare chest she'd been about to handle. "Forgive me. I didn't see you there."

"Obviously," she said. Her angry voice adjusted to a higher pitch. "It's my favorite dress."

With good reason. Neal made a note of the pronounced Russian accent. She squinted for a moment, a tiny spark of recognition lit and then faded. Her encounter that afternoon at the Mancuso mansion was causing her to mistrust everyone and see things that weren't there. "I'll buy you a new one," Neal said, scrambling to smooth things over before the woman caused a scene.

"You can't. It's vintage couture. It's the only one of its kind."

Neal caught the catch in her voice and realized she was genuinely upset. She couldn't imagine getting worked up about a piece of clothing, but rich people did a lot of things she couldn't relate to. The thought jogged a memory and she reached into her pocket, pulled out a wad of cash, and held it out. "I'm really very sorry. Maybe there's another one of a kind that would suit you just as well."

The woman's eyes widened slightly at the sight of the large bills. Probably wondering what she'd done to get that kind of cash. The answer was easy—absolutely nothing. She'd found the money in an envelope in Siobhan's apartment after she'd taken off with Royal. Her name graced the outside of the envelope in Siobhan's graceful, flowing script, but there was no note of explanation inside. Neal had taken it for safekeeping, but she'd never intended to use it. Paying for a ruined piece of fashion seemed as good a use for it as any. Especially if it made the Russian beauty stop throwing daggers her way.

"I don't need your money," the woman said.

"You don't look like you have need for many things."

The woman raised an eyebrow and cocked her head. "You are very presumptuous."

"I've had a hard week, and I don't have a lot of patience." On impulse, she stuck out her hand. "My name is Neal. It's nice to meet you."

A slight grin teased at the corner of the woman's lips as she looked down at Neal's outstretched hand. "Ah, you think it's nice to collide with total strangers and leave them in tatters?"

Neal let her gaze drift from the woman's face to her cleavage and back again. She was stunning. And she knew it, but the realization didn't keep Neal from appreciating the sight. "I don't see any signs of tatters here." Her pulse pounded as their eyes locked, and for a moment, everything else receded—the Don's death, Siobhan's departure, the attack on the Mancuso home, her complete and total lack of direction. All she could think about was kissing the ripe, red lips and—

"What's going on, Ana?"

The voice that ripped through her thoughts was harsh, but Neal was happy to have the information it conveyed. "Ana?"

The woman nodded in response before turning to the new arrival. "Katia, where have you been?"

"Flirting with one of the bartenders." She gestured vaguely in the direction of Honey's spot at the bar. "They are incorrigible." She turned to Neal. "I bet you already know that."

Neal resisted asking what that was supposed to mean. She was ready to end this conversation. "The more you come here, the less likely it'll be the bartenders hit you up for silly things."

"Are *you* hitting my friend up for silly things?" Katia asked, circling her like a cheetah.

Neal fixed her with a steely gaze. "Silly isn't my style, but if she'd like to join me for dinner sometime, that'd be fine by me."

"I bet it would."

She took note of the edge in Katia's voice while watching Ana's face, unable to get a read on her reaction. Probably for the best. She wasn't here to flirt or fuck or do anything other than find out if Siobhan had left any clues behind, likely a lost cause. She tore her gaze from Ana's and faced her protective companion.

"Not to worry. Dinner isn't really my thing." She gave a mock salute and walked away, resisting the urge to turn back for one more look at Ana in her pretty, albeit stained dress. She made a mental note to find a way to make it up to her, couture or not, and strode across the room, back to Honey who slid a drink her way the moment she reached the bar. She started to push the glass away, but decided she deserved a break and took a healthy swallow.

"I see you struck out with the ice women," Honey said. "Don't worry, you're not the only one."

"Hard to strike out when you're not playing." She risked a surreptitious glance across the room. "What's the story there?"

"The tall one's a mystery, but her sidekick comes in here every weekend. Kind of like your friend."

The word friend didn't define her relationship with Siobhan. Didn't come close. And Neal didn't appreciate the casual way Honey referred to her charge. She might be angry with Siobhan for abandoning her and the family business, but after years of dedicated service, she'd earned that right. Honey was a stranger and she had no business making judgments. She reached into her pocket for some cash and pulled out a few bills and shoved them toward Honey who looked surprised at the abrupt end to their conversation.

"Leaving?"

She froze at the sound of the silky voice and slowly turned to face Ana, sans her friend. She let her gaze roam slowly over Ana's entire body—a virtual embrace—savoring every second. Finally, she found words to match the feeling of desire welling up from within.

"Is there a reason I shouldn't?"

"No. Leaving is an excellent idea." Ana slipped an arm around her waist. "But there's no need to do it alone."

Neal breathed deep to keep from hyperventilating with excitement. What was wrong with her? She didn't indulge in the pleasures of this club as often as Siobhan, but she'd done her share of going home with beautiful women. Single episode encounters, designed for no attachment, no distraction. But this wasn't that, and she'd known it wouldn't be from the first moment she'd spotted Ana in the club. She shook her head. "I have to go."

Ana slid her hand up her back. "You do not have to do anything you do not want to do. For me. For anyone."

"If only it were that easy." Neal cocked her head. "I guess you've decided to forgive me for ruining your dress?"

A smile played lightly across Ana's lips. "Forgiveness is a process. Let's say I've taken the first step." She leaned in close, and her whisper was steamy against Neal's ear. "Would you like to help me take another?"

Neal stiffened with resistance, and then tried to figure out why. The temptation was great. This woman checked all the boxes. She was a total stranger and breathtakingly gorgeous. Besides, she could use some relief after the turmoil in the wake of Don Carlo's death. It wasn't like she'd seen anyone tonight who was going to lead her to Siobhan. Why not indulge her own fantasies for an evening instead of guarding someone else's?

She ran her hand down Ana's arm and threaded her fingers through hers. "Sure, why not?" Like it was the easiest decision in the world. And it was. Until she heard a man's voice behind her.

"So, this is where you play when I'm working."

Neal turned toward the loud, sharp voice and cringed with recognition. Mikhail Petrov, one of the Mancuso family's most formidable enemies, stood facing her, but his eyes were fixed firmly on Ana. It only took a second for Neal to grasp the gravity of what was happening. She resolved to play it cool. "Hello, Mikhail."

He pointed at her but directed his words to Ana. "See how this is? She knows my name. But I do not know hers. I don't need to know hers, because all I need to know is that she is loyal to my enemies. Isn't that right, dear?"

He punctuated his question by grabbing Ana around the waist and pulling her toward him. Neal watched Ana's face, certain she would win if she resisted, but she didn't put up any show of a fight other than a look of disdain. She'd only seen Petrov's wife one other time and only for a moment which explained why she hadn't realized who Ana was from the start. If she'd known, there wouldn't have been any flirtatious banter. No, she would've gotten the hell out of the bar.

Which begged the question: what was Anastasia Petrov doing in a queer bar?

❖

Ana hugged the door on her side of the limousine, determined to stay out of Mikhail's reach. Meanwhile, he acted like it didn't bother him at all to find her in a women's bar. It shouldn't—their attraction to women was the only thing they had in common.

"It doesn't bother me," he said, tipping a glass of icy Cristal to his lips and downing it in one gulp. "I trust you to bring home a beautiful specimen for both of us to enjoy."

She turned in her seat and stared out the window, refusing to take the bait.

"That one you were flirting with?" He growled. "She's not for you. Or anyone else. Women that tall are only good for one thing." He mimed dribbling a ball. "Like that athlete. The one who smuggled the drugs into Mother Russia."

Ana started to open her mouth to refute the faux news summary of Brittney Griner's plight, but she decided the energy would be a wasted effort. Mikhail was successful because of his muscle not his mind, and he didn't deal in nuance.

"You have nothing to say?" he asked.

The challenge in his voice was impossible to ignore. "I have a lot to say, but very little to you. You're drunk."

"You say that like it's a bad thing." He patted his chest. "You'd drink too if you were me. Married to a woman who doesn't know how to please."

She laughed. "I know how to please, but I'm particular about my pleasures. Not just any whore will do."

"That's rich. You would've left with that bitch if I hadn't shown up when I did." He grunted. "She's the bodyguard for Mancuso's consigliere. Likely left behind when the rest of the family fled the city after the old man died. She's either incredibly loyal or too dumb to realize when the fight is lost. Either way, she's not for you."

She tensed at his proclamation. He was constantly testing his power, likely hoping one day it might be enough to give him sway over her. It was wearing.

"You have no idea what you're talking about," she said. She pointed at him and back to her. "This is an arrangement. One you knew about from the start. You have the money and resources you were promised. Now you simply have to fulfill your part of the bargain and leave me alone. Understand?"

She could see the resignation in his eyes, but she also saw rebellion and a struggle to cede his manhood to get the other things he wanted. Not her problem. She'd married so their families could broker a business deal. As long as she stayed with him, the business would be successful, but if she left, it could all fall apart. Their relationship was the glue that kept everything together, but it was sticky at best.

When they arrived home, Mikhail retired to his overly ornate study where he spent his days intimidating everyone but her. He'd strut around, admiring all the silly things he collected and drink himself into a stupor like he did every night.

Grateful he was already too drunk to enforce their vows, she took the stairs to her private bedroom. Katia followed her, likely expecting to be invited in for a recap of the evening, but she feigned a headache and asked to be left alone for the rest of the evening. Her head might not hurt, but it was full. Images of Neal at the bar, looking rakishly handsome in an I-don't-really-care-about-impressing-anyone kind of way, standing up to Mikhail in a manner that none of the others who came to the house would dare to do paraded through her thoughts, but she pushed them away. She'd gone to the bar looking for release, not an encumbrance. If Neal really was connected to the Mancuso family, any connection would be complicated, and she had no interest in more complications. Even if they came in incredibly interesting packages.

CHAPTER FOUR

Neal stood in the stockroom and quietly assessed the rest of the group. A week ago, she would've considered every one of them loyal members of the family, but after Don Mancuso had been buried in the ground, she wasn't sure she could trust any of them.

It's not your place.

The voice in her head had been getting louder and louder, but she'd managed to keep it at bay. She had to because no one else was doing anything to try to wrangle this group, and she sensed rallying the forces was key to keeping things running until Siobhan returned and told them all what to do.

"What are we doing here?" Robert asked, his sullen tone signaling the mood of the group. Robert Valentino hadn't been a capo for long and he'd yet to learn that the chain of command didn't always run in a straight line. Her close association with Siobhan meant she was often in the room when big decisions were made which boosted her authority, a fact that gnawed at him and, she suspected, others in the room.

She started to answer him, but Michael punched him in the arm before she could reply. "We're here to listen." Michael glared at the assembled soldiers and then pointed at her. "The

Don left Siobhan in charge and Siobhan left Neal in charge. That's all you need to know. Now, pay attention and do what she says."

Robert looked down and shuffled his feet. Neal could tell he had more on his mind, and she couldn't really blame him. Their world had been blown apart with the death of the Don, and it wasn't like any of them realized why he had placed his consigliere in charge instead of one of his own family members because they hadn't heard Don's deathbed secret—Siobhan was his firstborn child, not Dominque. Speaking of which... She turned to Michael. "Anyone find out where Dominique is hiding out?"

He shook his head. "Working on it. Best guess is she left town."

"Let's not guess. I have a feeling she's nearby." She started to add, "waiting for her chance to exact revenge," but the fact the Don had cut Dominque from the family for her betrayal wasn't known to everyone in the group. Ironic that she knew more than these made men, and Muriel's words of advice echoed in her thoughts. Fine. She'd have to make her own way. Step up. Take charge. Whatever she had to do to preserve the legacy of the man who had saved her life and the woman whose life she'd been charged with protecting. Her gut clenched, but she was ready for the challenge. She took a moment to survey the assembled foot soldiers and decided to take a risk.

"Dominique has betrayed the family. I..." She glanced over at Michael who gave her a subtle nod. "We believe she's working with Mikhail Petrov. She pushed Don Carlo to adopt Petrov's business practices and it backfired." She conveniently left out the part about how Dominique probably had no idea she wasn't even the firstborn child of the family and unlikely to inherit on the level she expected, if at all. "She's been cut off from the family, but finding out where she is and what she's up to is critical."

"To who?"

She resisted turning toward the sound of Robert's sullen voice and she channeled her best impression of Siobhan with a calm, level voice. "To all of us."

"Family, my ass."

That's it. Time to punch this guy in the face because nothing else was going to get him to shut up. The pull was strong and she leaned into it, like an old friend who knew exactly what she needed. She turned and stalked toward him, determined to silence his doubts with her fists, but when she came to a stop a step from his face, the flicker of fear reflected in his eyes flooded her with a sense of calm. This guy's words meant nothing to her, to the family. Giving an ounce more of attention would only fuel his fire and deplete her own, and she didn't have time for that. She didn't need to resort to actual violence if he or anyone else inclined to challenge her believed she'd follow through when pushed. Good thing since she'd need every warm body in this room to resist the assault from Petrov's goons.

An image of Anastasia flashed in her mind. What role did she play in Petrov's power games? She'd always been reclusive—the polar opposite of her showy husband, who enjoyed rolling up to clubs in chauffeur-driven limousines and ordering bottle service in velvet-roped VIP lounges with scantily-clad women fawning over him and his friends, while Ana, in her understated vintage couture, seemed more concerned with blending in. Not that anyone that beautiful had any hope of fading into the background.

Not her concern why those two opposites attracted, and Ana shouldn't be her concern at all unless she could tie her to Mikhail's offensive against the Mancusos. She shook her head. Didn't seem likely. No, not at all.

A light touch against her arm brought her back to the matters at hand and she looked up to see the assembled group staring at her. She took a step back from Robert but shot him a withering look to punctuate her disdain. Once she was back at the edge of the room where she could take in everyone's faces, she cleared her throat. "This is what's going to happen. We're at war. I want two things." She shot out a finger. "Find Dominique. She needs to answer for her betrayal, but more importantly, we need to make sure she isn't burning off the family assets." She flipped another finger at the group. "Next, we need to shore up support. Reach out to everyone who owes us. Confirm their allegiance, and if they waver..." She paused and waited a few beats to emphasize her point. "You know what to do."

No one spoke and everyone stayed frozen in place. She let them digest her words for a moment and then waved her arm in the air. "Go. Git. You'll hear from Michael when it's time to check in."

They practically ran from the room, likely relieved to be dismissed. Hopefully, they'd come back when called instead of trading loyalties to a family that might look like they were falling apart.

Once the door shut behind them, she turned to Michael. "We need to talk."

❖

Ana brushed out her hair and winced as she struck another knot. She'd slept fitfully and the dark circles under her eyes and tangled hair were the least of it. Her encounter with Neal at the bar and the subsequent dealing with Mikhail's bullshit he-man routine had her on edge and her mind had churned through the night, keeping her awake. She was so tired now, she didn't see Katia walk into the room.

"Did you really sleep down here?" Katia asked, referring to her private suite, located in the opposite end of the house from Mikhail's quarters.

"Sleep didn't factor in, unfortunately." She flicked a glance at the door. "He was in a mood."

"He's always in a mood. You must truly love him to put up with it. You could have anyone you want."

Katia delivered the words with a smoldering look and Ana glanced away. A moment later, she felt Katia's hand on hers.

"Don't worry. You're safe with me."

She shuddered at the words. An echo of the sworn promise Mikhail had made on their wedding day. She didn't pay attention to the meaning then, mostly because all she could think about was that marriage ceremonies shouldn't have anything to do with safety, only love. But what did she know? She'd never had the chance to explore the only kind of love she wanted. Her destiny wasn't designed for personal success.

"Are you okay?"

The voice sounded far away, but she turned to it just the same. Katia stared into her eyes with intense and genuine concern, and Ana forced herself not to look away. She cared about Katia, but she would never take things further than the friendship they shared because friendship was all she felt for her, and she wasn't cruel enough to indulge her desires at the expense of Katia's feelings. She shrugged. "I am. Only tired and that will pass. We have some work to do."

Katia raised her eyebrows and walked to the door. She leaned into the hallway outside of Ana's suite and then quietly shut the door. When she turned back to Ana, she wore a mischievous grin. "I have a feeling you're going to want to keep this between us."

Ana returned the grin. "You'd be right about that." She pointed to her desk on the other side of the room. "I spent most of the night running numbers. Mikhail is bleeding through our money like there's an infinite supply. If he thinks my family is going to support his alliances with people who are only going to dwindle their fortune, then he is in for a rude awakening."

Katia swept across the room and pointed to the desk. "You shouldn't keep these papers here. If Mikhail sees them in your room." She shook her head. "He's not a forgiving sort."

"Neither am I." She delivered the words with a stern tone which belied her true situation. As long as her fate was tied to Mikhail, her power was limited, and everyone knew it. Her family didn't approve of him personally, but the benefits of their alliance allowed them to have political influence which outweighed any of his unsavory traits. But if he was draining them financially, would they feel the same way?

She reached for the envelope she'd sealed late last night when she'd tired of tossing and turning. The letter inside was a recitation of facts, persuasively crafted to convince her family Mikhail was a danger to not only their fortune, but power they craved. She'd written the letter in anger, but everything in it was true. Her only fear was that it would not be enough. Mikhail had been tasked with infiltrating the other powerful families in this area, taking over their business or building alliances where full control wasn't possible. He'd likely aligned with someone to take the Mancusos down and it was draining their resources, but without knowing who his allies were, she didn't have much chance of convincing anyone of the danger of his actions.

She pushed the envelope back into the drawer and slid it shut. The time for Mikhail's reckoning would come soon enough, but she needed better intelligence to ensure he would be out of her life forever, and she wasn't convinced a letter was a strong enough weapon. In the meantime, she needed to create some alliances of her own. She looked up at Katia who stared at her with a curious expression. She had to trust someone and it might as well be her. "I need a favor."

"Anything," Katia answered quickly, eagerly. "You know I'm here for you."

Ana took a deep breath and braced for her pushback. "I need you to arrange a meeting with Neal Walsh."

Katia looked puzzled at first, but then anger flashed across her face. "Siobhan Collin's bodyguard? The woman from Sanctuary?"

"Yes."

"Mikhail will lose his mind."

"Mikhail has already lost his mind, which is precisely why I want this meeting." She fixed Katia with a hard stare. "You promised me 'anything.' What does that mean to you?"

Katia sat still for a moment and Ana watched the parade of emotions play out until resignation settled in. "Of course, I'll arrange the meeting. I only meant to point out the danger. You want me to look out for your interests, don't you?"

Ana studied her for a moment before replying. She knew deep down Katia would truly do anything for her, but she also knew Katia's loyalty was fueled by a desire to be something more than a friend and confidant which meant her motivation could turn if she felt she were being cut out of the equation. It was a balancing act for both of them because without Katia, she'd be left completely to her own devices to navigate her way out of her marriage to Mikhail. She had no other friends here and she didn't know how to make them in the shadow of Mikhail's enterprises. Anyone she met through their business connections would be tainted by their connection to Mikhail, and she rarely had the opportunity to venture out on her own except for an occasional visit to clubs like Sanctuary where the setting was designed for release, not forging alliances.

Perhaps Neal could prove to be both. Was she playing with fire? Perhaps, but she had to do something or she would burn in the flames of Mikhail's meltdown.

CHAPTER FIVE

Neal looked up at the knock on the door and shot a glance at Michael who'd been lounging on the couch across the room. She'd taken up residence in the manager's office at Valentino's, a large but unassuming liquor store that served as the base of operations for the Mancusos' operations. Michael had assumed the role of her bodyguard—a fact she hadn't quite adjusted to yet, but his presence gave her peace and she needed all the peace she could get as she tried to formulate a plan to combat the forces hard at work against the Mancuso family businesses.

She rose from her chair, but Michael was already at the door, gun drawn. "Who is it?" he barked.

"I have a message for Neal."

Neal recognized the voice immediately. She sounded like Ana, but her tone was more clipped and formal. She searched her mind for the name…Katherine, no, Katia. She signaled to Michael. "Let her in."

His furrowed brow signaled he disagreed with the decision, but he did as he was instructed and eased the door open, gun still drawn. A moment later, Katia strode into the room, breezy and confident, stopping directly in front of her desk. It had been almost a week since she'd met Ana and Katia at Club Sanctuary, and Katia looked as displeased here in her office as she had when they'd last met. She was beautiful—anyone would agree, but her beauty paled next to Ana's who was regal in comparison.

Focus. Beautiful women were distractions. Katia was here for something, and her connection to the Petrovs made her dangerous which meant her ability to distract could be deadly. Neal studied her for a moment before pointing at the chair in front of her desk. "Have a seat."

Katia looked at the aging leather chair with disgust. She pulled a handkerchief from her bag and wiped it down before settling into the seat. When she was settled, she leaned back and surveyed the room. "Not the most impressive of headquarters. You are in charge now?"

Neal refused to take the bait and merely responded, "You are not a very good spy. Perhaps you should be more subtle."

"I'm not here to spy, but if I was, I could report back that the Mancusos must be desperate to put you in charge. Weren't you nothing more than a bodyguard for the family lawyer?"

Diminishing her role reinforced Neal's own doubts, but she wasn't about to let Katia know that. "If you have business with the family, you can talk to me. Consider me a gatekeeper if you will. You'll have to be a lot more than a family friend of the Petrovs to get past the gate."

"Oh, I'm not trying to crash any gates. I'm only here to see you." She paused as if trying to decide what to say next. "Ana would like to meet with you. It must be in private. I'm sure you can understand and will respect the need for privacy."

Doubt crept up Neal's spine with icy fingers. "Tell her she can find what she needs back at the club. I'm not interested."

Katia laughed. "You needn't worry. Ana's inquiry is strictly professional." She paused and leaned in. "Though I have no idea why she believes you would be the one to trust. Perhaps you will be a good messenger to whoever is in charge of what is left of this…" She looked around with a disgusted expression. "Enterprise."

The bait was too much this time. Neal rose. "Tell your friend I'm not interested in talking to the wife of a madman. Where I come from, we judge people by the company they keep, and Mrs. Petrov has failed supremely in that department."

Katia stood. "Perfectly acceptable to me. I told her this overture was a waste of time." She placed a card on the desk. "If you change your mind, call that number." She paused. "I hope you don't."

She sailed out the door without waiting for an answer. Michael shut the door behind her and paced the room. Neal recognized his method of thinking things out and she was certain he had something to say about how she'd handled the meeting with Katia. "Please sit down. You're making me crazy. And you may as well go ahead and tell me what's on your mind."

"Not my place," he grumbled under his breath.

"I'm telling you it's your place. I'm not in charge here, no matter what we want the rest of the crew to think. If you have something to say, speak."

"We're in trouble here. The only real alliance we have to speak of is the Casey family and they're a state away dealing with their own shit. The wife of the Don's sworn enemy sends a messenger to set up a meeting and you toss her out. Did it occur to you that she's going behind her husband's back? That she may have her own reasons to forge an alliance with us?"

It hadn't. All she could think of when she heard Katia's message was that she was being lured into a trap. That Petrov was using the attraction he'd witnessed at Sanctuary between her and Ana to compromise her, to gain an edge. She was seeing only trees when there was an entire forest to navigate. "I suck at this."

"You don't, but you have to think differently than you're used to. You're used to protecting the physical well-being of this family, but Don Carlo is dead, Siobhan is with Royal, Dominique has betrayed us, and Celia has her husband to watch out for her. Your job now is to hold things together until Siobhan comes home, and that means exploring every angle."

He was right, of course. "You sound like a consigliere."

"You should know. You were in the room almost every time Siobhan advised the Don. Why do you think she left you in charge?"

That was the big question. The one that had had her on edge for days. All she'd ever been was a bodyguard and security was her only angle. A private meeting with Anastasia Petrov was the least secure thing she could do right now. But what if meeting with Ana helped her garner more information about what Mikhail was up to? That kind of intel would help her formulate strategy, prove her worth. She could use a little worth since right now she was a bodyguard with no one to protect. If Siobhan thought she could handle being in charge, then it was time to put her theory to the test.

"I don't know why I'm in charge, but as long as I am, let's go ahead and set up the meeting."

Michael grinned. "That's great, boss. I'll make sure it's a safe place. We won't let anything happen to you. I promise." She heard his words, but instead of being reassuring, they transported her back in time.

She heard the crack of the bat, but it took a moment for the pain to register, for her to connect the sickening sound with the sharp, piercing pain across her back. When it did she pressed her fist into her mouth and fought against the urge to howl. Her cries would only egg him on.

"All you had to do was foul out, but no...you decide you want to be the goddamned player of the week."

A steel toe punctuated each word, and despite her best efforts, she groaned in agony. "Don't you have anything to say, bitch?"

She had plenty to say, but the blinding pain made it hard to speak. She'd started tonight's game with every intention of keeping her agreement to throw it to the other team, but two minutes after the tip-off, she changed her mind. She'd spent her entire youth being made fun of for her height, and basketball was her only revenge. This team, this school, this scholarship were accomplishments she'd worked hard to achieve, and if she could stick it out, she could figure out a way to help her family without throwing it all away.

"Not a quitter." She choked out the words between ragged breaths, bracing for his response.

"Great. Because you won't be able to quit this."

She watched the bat rush through the air toward her leg, but with his foot on her torso, she was powerless to get out of the way. When the weapon connected, the pain before felt like a caress compared to the white-hot burn of agony roaring up from her shattered leg. She wailed in agony.

She ripped her thoughts from the memory but rubbed her leg as if it was still in pain. She hadn't been able to protect herself then, what made her think she could protect an entire empire now?

CHAPTER SIX

Y ou're sure she said she would come?" Ana stared at the door of the restaurant for the dozenth time, irritated at her own agitation. She was the one holding court here, not Neal, but she couldn't help but feel like she was an anxious suitor, hoping her date would show.

"She'll be here," Katia said. "She's curious and not smart or subtle enough to strategize some other way to obtain information. Trust me."

Ana nodded at the trust me part, but she balked inwardly at Katia's assessment of Neal. True, they'd only spent a few moments together at Sanctuary, but her first impression of Neal was that she was sharp and quick-witted, not a stereotypical dumb athlete like Katia and Mikhail seemed to think.

Former athlete. Ana had found quite a few references to Neal's exemplary college basketball career, but the facts were scant and every article ended with some statement about what a shame it had been that she was no longer able to play with veiled references to injuries that had occurred off the court. More googling didn't yield any additional facts, and she'd decided she'd simply ask the source if she was still curious by the time Neal showed up.

If she showed up.

The waiter appeared and asked if she wanted to hear the specials. He mistook her murmur for assent and started reciting a long list of drinks and their respective ingredients. Several drinks in, she shot a look at Katia, who shooed him away, and she resumed her uncomfortable wait. "Five more minutes. If she doesn't show, we leave." She looked up in time to see Neal headed toward them. "Don't turn around, but she just walked in."

Katia immediately turned in her chair, and Ana whispered, "I said don't turn around."

"She can see you looking at her."

"Much different than having both of us stare. Of course she's used to being admired for her physicality, but we're not here to discuss that." Unless it comes up naturally she mused. As Neal took the final few steps to their table, Ana straightened in her seat and crossed her hands on the table. A moment later, Neal was towering next to her.

"Interesting place," Neal said. "Is this where you have all your assignations?"

Ana forced a laugh, like meeting other women for strategy sessions or anything else was a regular occurrence, and she was completely indifferent to Neal's allure. "Maybe. I suppose you'll have to follow me to find out." She gestured to the chair across from hers and Neal sat down, but even seated, she towered over the two of them. Ana waited a moment for Katia to excuse herself from the table, and then cocked her head. "Have you been following me?"

She was kidding, but the slight twitch along Neal's jaw told her she was on to something. "You *have* been following me. You must find it very boring."

Neal laughed. "Hardly. Although you don't leave the house much."

"Understatement."

"True. A little shopping and a luncheon now and then. Word is you go to the salon once a month." Neal tapped her fingers on the table. "I think that's it."

Ana resisted breathing a sigh of relief that Neal hadn't mentioned her other regular activity and simply smiled. "You're thorough."

"I am."

"An admirable quality."

"Is that why you asked me here today? Because you admire me?"

"I hardly know you."

"So that's why I was lucky enough to get the invite," Neal said. "You want to get to know me."

Neal grinned and Ana smiled back at her in return. She liked that Neal wasn't intimidated by her, that she seemed completely at ease. At home, Mikhail surrounded them with supplicants, as if his worth rose with every compliment, but she had no use for their sucking up. She knew her worth even if she'd chosen to trade it for a life with a soulless man and an empty marriage. Someday…hopefully soon, she'd find a way to trade it all away for exactly what she needed. "Maybe I want you to get to know me."

"I've barely spent any time with you, but already I see that you're a dreamer."

She balked at Neal's words, both irritated and intrigued at the characterization. "Dreams are for people who have no ambition."

Neal frowned. "Do you really believe that?"

"Why do you ask?" Ana sucked in a breath. "Wait, does the bodyguard dream of being someone else, not to mention somewhere and with some other people?"

"I'm not a bodyguard."

"Only because your charge has fallen out of favor and has crawled off to hide out until the storm dies down. Did she ask you before she left you alone to pick up the pieces?" She watched Neal shift in her seat, clearly uncomfortable with her assessment. Good. That made them even. She shook her head. "Never mind. Don't answer that. I'm sure she had her reasons."

Neal's lips parted and she inched forward in her seat, like she wanted to say something, but after a few seconds, she folded her arms and leaned back. "Everyone has reasons for the actions they take. Like you, for instance. Care to discuss why you summoned me to this meeting?"

This was it. The tipping point. In order to ask the question and get the information she wanted, she was going to have to divulge information, share secrets, strategically. Ana cleared her throat and reached for the glass of water at her place setting. After a deep swallow, she set the glass down and adjusted the coaster, not stalling so much as judging the best way to pitch her plan. When she looked up, Neal was staring at her with a smoldering intensity, belying the business nature of this meeting, and a surge of warmth flooded her. Why couldn't the liaison from the other side be less attractive, less desirable? Lust wasn't ideal when it came to employing strategy, but her options were limited.

"I have a business proposition."

Neal's gaze didn't waver, but Ana spotted a flash of interest in her eyes, which encouraged her to go on. "I believe Mikhail is working with Dominique Mancuso."

Neal lifted her glass and took a drink and Ana recognized the tactic. She waited patiently for Neal to digest the information and respond. She didn't have to wait long.

"So, what if he is?"

Not the response she'd expected. She'd been operating under the assumption Dominique's actions were independent of the rest of the Mancuso empire, but when it came down to it, she'd based her beliefs on Mikhail's reports—not her best move. She could either tuck tail or press on. There was really only one choice, and she decided to go all in. "If you don't realize Dominique is your enemy, then you have no business purporting to be in charge."

She watched carefully, but Neal's reaction was a small series of micro expressions—widening eyes, a slight twitch of her eyebrows, and her lips pressed together—but the rest of her body appeared relaxed and nonchalant.

"I assume your *belief*," Neal over-emphasized the word, "is based on facts, but the bigger question is why are you telling me this?" She raised her hands. "I'm not in charge of anything. Just an unemployed bodyguard, remember?"

"Maybe. Maybe that's simply what you'd like everyone to believe." Ana cleared her throat and dove in. "Whether you're in charge or simply the messenger, you should know that Mikhail has a grand plan to bring the Mancuso family business to its knees. Whose side are you on?"

Neal forced herself to stay calm, to keep her expression firmly fixed in neutral mode. This was the tip-off, right before the ref threw the ball into the air. She always knew exactly where she was headed, but hiding her plan from her opponent was key to her team's success.

This evening had all the trappings of a date. White linen tablecloths, candles, and fancy china. She'd accompanied Siobhan to many such places, but she'd never had a seat at the table. Instead, she'd been positioned nearby, ready for any trouble that might develop, well-placed to listen in, observe, but not participate in important family decisions. Not for the first time, she questioned Muriel's message. Had Siobhan really left her in charge, or had she abandoned the family entirely and left her behind only to cover her retreat?

She breathed deep. It didn't matter either way. She owed Don Carlo her life and she wasn't about to leave his legacy in tatters if there was any way around it. She faced Ana and delivered her message with intense calm. "If you know anything about me, then you know whose side I'm on."

Ana nodded like she respected the declaration. "Then I have a proposal. Would you like to hear what I have to say?"

The question seemed silly on its face, but it signaled to Neal that Ana was smart and savvy about the connections she was seeking to forge. Once Ana told her what she'd come to say, Neal wouldn't be able to unhear the words. Even if she didn't act on them, anyone else who found out about this meeting, about what they discussed would make assumptions about her loyalties and act accordingly. But here she was, sitting at a fancy restaurant with the wife of one of the most powerful crime organizations in Dallas, and there was no turning back now. She shrugged to convey a nonchalance she didn't feel, but she knew would be critical to whatever happened next. "Sure. I mean, I'm here already, right?"

The waiter showed up again and topped off their wine. He pointed at the menus they'd laid to the side. Neal started to say she wasn't hungry, but Ana spoke first.

"Bring us two filets, rare. A selection of sides, and another bottle of red. And leave us to talk." She looked at Neal. "You eat meat, right?"

The question was an afterthought, and from anyone else, Neal might have been offended at the assumption of control, but she found it admirable instead. She'd always assumed Mikhail's reclusive wife would either be exactly like one of the bimbos that accompanied him to clubs or a passive, milquetoast female he'd aligned with for family fortune, but Ana was a smart, passionate, beautiful specimen, the likes of which an ass like Mikhail would never deserve. "Yes, I eat meat." She turned to the waiter. "Make mine a ribeye. And I'd like a whiskey, neat." No sense letting Ana think she had all the control.

Ana watched the waiter leave and then turned back to her. "You like to act rough around the edges or is that really who you are?"

"We're not here to talk about me," Neal said. "I thought you wanted to tell me about your husband."

"Mikhail, yes."

Neal noted the sidestep. "He is your husband, isn't he?"

Ana grimaced. "We have an arrangement. You people here in the States do not understand true alliances. In my country, alliances are formed in childhood. My family matched me to Mikhail from a very young age."

"You're telling me you don't love him."

"Love? Love has nothing to do with relationships. Relationships are based on mutually beneficial connections, and the best ones have to do with business. When those desires no longer match, the relationship must end."

Neal thought about Siobhan's relationship with Royal, the FBI agent who'd been investigating the Mancuso family before things had shifted dramatically, and she'd abandoned her career to start a life with the consigliere of a crime family. Their attraction hadn't been about business at all, but apparently, Ana and Mikhail didn't have any connection outside of business. She filed that thought away to examine further when she was by herself. "I get it. You and Mikhail have different interests. How does that affect me?"

"I suppose it depends on what you want. Your Don is dead and your boss has fled the country." She arched her eyebrows. "Don't look surprised that I know this."

Neal cursed inwardly at her inability to mask emotion in Ana's presence. "It's not a secret that the situation is not ideal, but I am still curious about your angle in all this."

"Mikhail is making moves. Moves that place our assets at risk. I may have tied my fate to him, but I will not go down for his mistakes. The Mancusos have a cash flow problem and I have ready access to plenty of funds. Funds that will allow you to reclaim your stakes and rebuild."

"What do you get out of it?"

"What do you care if my help gets you what you need?"

Neal sighed, disappointed that Ana so clearly underestimated her. She shoved back from the table. "Find someone else to help you find a way out of your marriage. Or better yet, find your own way. Not everyone has a secret fortune at their disposal—don't act so helpless."

She turned to walk away, but Ana's commanding tone stopped her before she'd made a single step.

"Secret fortunes aren't any good without alliances. I'm offering you more than money here."

Neal was certain Ana was referring to business, but her suggestive tone was a lure that kept her fixed in place. She wanted her to ask what the "more than" was, but if she did, she'd be headed down this road without any sense of direction. She should leave. Go back to Michael and the rest of the crew and dig in until they figured a way to keep things together until Siobhan came back or Dominique came to her senses. The Mancusos had ruled Dallas for many years, and they'd find a way to seize control again.

Or not.

What would become of her then? She'd only ever known two career paths in her life: basketball and working for the Mancuso family. There was no college degree or family to fall back on. Add to that the fact there were people who relied on her, who wouldn't survive without the money she wired every month, funds she had because of her position. The cash flow problem wasn't just the Mancusos', it was hers as well.

She slowly turned back to Ana and placed her hand on the back of the chair she'd just abandoned. "I'll stay, under one condition."

Ana motioned for her to sit. "Name it."

Motive was everything and Neal needed to know Ana's before she could trust her, align with her in any way. "Tell me what's in it for you."

Ana sighed and looked away for a moment. When she turned back, her smile was melancholy. "I could easily make up some lie. Something plausible you would believe in order to get you to work with me. I won't do that. It's disrespectful. It's not a good way to start a relationship. I can only promise you this. Someday, I will tell you, but now is not the time."

Neal shifted in her seat at the way Ana said the word "relationship," but then again everything Ana said sounded sexy and suggestive. She forced her attention back to Ana's refusal to declare her motive, a move that should end this discussion, make her walk away, but she didn't do either. Siobhan had left her in charge. Michael believed she could handle it, but she was certain he said that because he thought it was temporary. She had an opportunity here to forge her own alliance, bring something of great value to the table. This gig might be temporary, but what if she could leave a lasting impression? Besides, she owed it to Siobhan to step up—this was another way of protecting the family, every bit as important as being a bodyguard.

"Fine, but you better keep your promise." She leaned in close to Ana. "Tell me more about this alliance."

Chapter Seven

It had been over a week, nine days to be exact, and Neal hadn't heard a single word from Ana. She was beginning to think their encounter had been a figment of her imagination, but Michael assured her he'd seen the entire dinner take place from his spot across the dining room. Maybe it was only the content of the conversation her memory hadn't accurately captured.

Yet, Ana hadn't called, hadn't sent any messages. So much for their mutually beneficial arrangement. Hard to have one of those when one party ghosted the other.

"Boss, there's a truck outside. Driver says it's an order for you."

Neal shook off her malaise and stared at Michael who was standing in the door to the manager's office at Valentino's. She hadn't placed any orders since it was unlikely anyone would leave the booze with no cash in hand—a theory she had no plans to test in front of any of the rest of the crew who didn't have personal knowledge of the extent of the financial problems that faced them all. If they knew how little cash the family had on hand, they would panic, and Neal needed everyone to remain calm and focused on the business, not jumping ship because they thought it was going under.

She walked out of the building and onto the dock to find a large trailer backed up to the first of three loading docks. A guy she assumed was the driver was leaned against the back doors of the trailer holding a clipboard.

"You Neal?" he asked.

Hardly any of the suppliers knew her well enough to recognize her in person. She ignored the question and pointed at the clipboard. "That your order?"

"Yep."

She held out a hand and he shoved it toward her. She stared at the contents for a moment, and then began flipping pages, but they all looked the same, each listing case after case of liquor. "We didn't order all this." She turned another page. "We didn't order any of it."

The driver hunched his shoulders. "It's paid for and I'm supposed to deliver it here." He glanced at his watch. "I got another delivery to make. Tell me where you want me to unload."

Another warning bell went off in Neal's head. The Mancusos had never paid invoices in advance. Something was up.

As if on cue, her phone buzzed, signaling an incoming text. *Accept the gift and consider it a show of good faith. You'll hear from me soon.*

She didn't recognize the number, but she knew exactly who'd sent the message. Years of hard-earned cynicism urged her to send the truck away, but her gut told her to heed Ana's message and see where it led. She pointed to the left side of the warehouse. "You can unload over there. Make sure the boxes stay separate from the ones already there."

She watched him unload, scrutinizing the outside of the boxes as if they contained important clues. The free booze was a nice gesture, but it would only exacerbate the cash flow problem since they'd have to sell it to make money and they were already having trouble unloading the inventory they had on hand. Whatever. So Ana didn't have a great business mind. It wasn't like she'd expected to hear from her at all.

"What's with the boxes?" Michael asked, appearing at her side.

"Good question. Apparently, our new friend thinks we don't have booze to fill all our orders." She fished out her pocketknife and reached for the closest box. "At least we'll have a bigger profit margin since this is all gratis." She slid the knife along the box tape and peeled back the lid to reveal a dozen bottles of Jameson's. She reached a hand in the box. "May as well take a couple to have in the office." Her fingers curled around the neck of the bottle, but when she went to lift it, her hand flung through the air as it weighed much less than she expected. "What the hell?"

"What is it?" Michael asked.

"Not sure." She turned the label and stared at the print. It looked real, but even through the green glass she could tell there was no liquid in the bottle, only a thick, brick shaped object. She reached for the cap and started to turn it, listening for the sound of a broken seal. Nothing. She twisted it the rest of the way off and turned the bottle upside down.

"Seriously, Neal," Michael said. "What're you doing?" His eyes widened when nothing came out of the bottle. "Empties?"

She shook it and listened to the thunk of whatever was inside. "No, but no liquor for sure." She shook the bottle hard. Nothing came out, but she felt a seam in the glass with the tip of her finger. She examined it for a moment, impressed by the length someone had gone to tuck away whatever was inside. Ana. She'd done this. Her impression of Petrov's trophy wife rose even further.

But this wasn't about being impressed. Her impression of Ana would only get in the way of any potential business relationship. She hefted the bottle and looked around the room. "Stand back." She barely waited for Michael to get out of the way before striking the bottle against one of the steel support beams nearby. It broke at the seam, and a sparkly mess of jade shattered and scattered around her boots. But it wasn't the green that caught her eye. "Cash," she murmured. "She sent cash." She reached down, brushed away shards of glass, and flipped through the stack of banded bills.

"This from Petrov's wife?" Michael asked. "There's like fifty g's in that bottle alone. How the hell did they get it in there?"

The words "Petrov's wife" rubbed her the wrong way, but she pushed her annoyance away in favor of figuring out exactly what Ana had done. She pointed to the rest of the boxes. "Check them. Just you."

"You want me to break any cash out of the bottles?"

"Nope. You see any more like this, put them back like you never saw them. Sometimes the best hiding place is in plain sight. Just check every case and report back if you find anything like what we just saw."

"Roger that." He was a couple of steps from the door when he paused and turned back. "What does she want for all this?"

Exactly the question that had been rocking around in her head. "I have no idea, but I'm thinking whatever she wants is a big ask or she wouldn't be risking her marriage, let alone her life. Whatever it is, we'll deal with it when the time comes. In the meantime, everything about these boxes is top secret—where they came from, what's in them. You and me are in the know, but no one else. Got it?"

"Got it."

She nodded and walked to her office, resisting the pull of helping Michael catalogue the funds, but the guys couldn't see her doing menial work in the warehouse because it would diminish her authority. Laughing, talking, and being part of the group—she'd lost all of that when she agreed to be in charge, but someone had to lead and, despite the fact she'd never wanted the job, it was hers now and she'd rise to it, like she'd always done in the past.

Neal nearly dropped the pan at the sound of a knock on the door. The only person who ever knocked was the deadbeat landlord who expected rent on time but never fixed a damn thing until time had run out on it. It was the fifteenth—what could he want smack in the middle of the month?

She set the pan down and wiped her hands on the kitchen towel, steeling herself for a difficult conversation. She strode to the door and cracked it as far as the chain lock would allow, but it wasn't her fat, bearded landlord standing in the hall. No, it was the tall, svelte beauty who'd been with Don Carlo the night he'd rescued her from being beaten to death by Fellini's guys.

"Take off the chain and let me in."

The woman's commanding tone gave off the impression she was used to being obeyed, which naturally made Neal want to resist. She spent a moment considering the consequences before finally slipping the chain from the lock and pulling back the door to let the woman in. No matter how much she didn't want a stranger in her house, she'd pledged her loyalty to Don Carlo and anyone who worked for him with no exceptions for bossy women who showed up on her doorstep late at night, and then made themselves at home the way this woman was doing right now.

"I never got your name," Neal said as she followed the woman into the living room. Seeing the room through a stranger's eyes, she was struck by how much tinier it was than anything this woman was probably used to.

"I never said my name."

"I guess that explains that. Tell me now."

"Are you always this demanding?" the woman asked. "Because that could pose a problem."

"For who?"

"My name is Siobhan," the woman said, kind of answering the question. She walked in a circle around Neal and made clicking sounds with her tongue. "It's nice to see a woman taller than I am."

Neal pointed at the tall stilts that Siobhan was wearing. "What are those? Three inches? Four? Pretty sure you don't have to be as tall as you are. Me? I'm stuck this way."

"You say that like it's a bad thing."

"It's only good for one thing and that thing is dead to me now."

Siobhan nodded. "True. You'll never play college ball again, let alone pro, but that's not the only avenue left to you."

The honesty was harsh but refreshing, especially since everyone else in her life kept assuring her she'd return to the sport someday. "I'm aware I'll never play again. And I know I can do pretty much anything else, but nothing where I blend in, where it's perfectly normal to be this tall."

"Blending in can be overrated."

"Said people who have no trouble doing it." *Neal walked to the kitchen only half caring if Siobhan would follow her. She was starving and her omelet was getting cold. She looked behind her to find Siobhan standing less than a foot away.* "Are you hungry?"

"Maybe."

"If that 'maybe' is because you think I can't cook, you'd be mistaken. I'm no chef, but I can make a decent omelet and I'm starving. You can either watch me or join me." *She reached for the pan and slid the omelet onto a plate, sliced it in half, and slid one of the halves onto another plate which she shoved toward Siobhan.* "Enjoy."

Siobhan stared at the food for a moment before picking up a fork and taking a bite. "Not bad." *She poked around with her fork.* "Spinach, tomatoes, mushrooms, cheese. Garlic too, right?"

Neal smiled. "Garlic is my favorite food group. You like?"

"I do. My mother was the head cook for the Mancuso family for many years and she never shied away from flavor."

Interesting. Neal would've never guessed that the consigliere for a powerful Don would confess her mother had worked as a servant, but then again, she never would've expected Mancuso's consigliere to show up at her doorstep either. She wanted to drill deeper, find out what this visit was all about, but sensed it would be best to let Siobhan get to the point when she was ready, so she dove into her half of the omelet while she waited for this scene to play out.

"Do you cook for your sister?"

Neal nearly choked on her food at Siobhan's question—both for the content and the breezy way she asked, like it was no big deal that Siobhan knew she had a sister, that she took care of her. She decided the best thing to do was to match Siobhan's nonchalant tone. "I used to, but there are people who cook for her now. I guess you already know that."

Siobhan nodded and took another bite. She wiped her lips and managed to make the simple act incredibly sexy.

Watch yourself. *Before she could focus too much on the thought, Siobhan spoke again.*

"You don't visit her much anymore."

Neal's gut clenched with guilt and the disturbing realization Siobhan knew way more about her than most people. Was she being judged? Would she fall short? Did she care?

After a moment, she decided to meet the comment head-on. "It's easier on everyone if I don't."

"Hmm." Siobhan finished off her omelet and dabbed at her lips with her napkin before folding it neatly and setting it to the side of the plate. "Does your mother know what you did?"

She shook her head. She hadn't confided in her about the deal she'd struck with the Fellini family to throw the last round of the tournament, trading her chance at a championship ring for a better life for her sister. Ida Walsh didn't have the capacity or motivation to take the lead, so it had been up to her. Now that everything had worked out there was no sense filling in the details, details she'd have questions about and wouldn't be able to let go.

"You did the right thing. She would never understand," Siobhan said, eerily echoing her thoughts.

"How do you know so much about it?"

Siobhan's expression softened for a moment. "I too have made hard choices. Choices that were very personal and private."

Neal was sure this was meant to be a kumbaya moment, but she was ready to get back to her evening, and it didn't involve cyphering cryptic messages from a counselor to a mob family even if that very family had saved her life. She may be alive and her sister cared for, but she'd lost everything else and there was no way back from that. *"The difference between us is that you get to keep your choices private. The end of my career is all over the news."* She pointed at the boot she wore on her right foot. *"And this is my daily reminder. Did you come here to rub it in?"*

"You have an interesting way of thanking your benefactors."

Neal bowed her head at the scolding. She knew she should be grateful, but worry over what her future held clouded her thoughts, stoked her rebellion. She mustered a trace of humility. *"I'm sorry. I owe Don Carlo a debt and I will gladly repay."*

Siobhan stood, reached into her bag, and pulled out a keycard. *"Good."* She handed Neal the card. *"I'll text you my address and this will get you into the building. There's a seven a.m. flight to Dallas, and you can take a cab from Love Field. Be at my place by nine a.m."* She didn't wait for a response before starting toward the door.

Neal stared at the card in her hand. She may owe a debt, but that didn't mean she'd signed up to be this woman's

*plaything, let alone move to another state to be at her disposal.
"Wait." Siobhan turned in time to see her toss the card on the
kitchen counter. "I'm not interested."*

*Siobhan looked at the card and then stared hard at her in
total silence for what seemed like forever. When she spoke, her
words were sharp and clipped. "It wasn't a request. You need
a job and I need a bodyguard. Nine tomorrow. Don't be late."*

*Siobhan strode to the door and, this time, she didn't look
back. Neal watched her go while her mind swirled with the
import of what had just happened and how her life was about
to change.*

CHAPTER EIGHT

Ana took the martini from the handsome butch bartender and sipped the smooth icy vodka like it would soothe her soul. And it almost did. But vodka wasn't quite enough anymore to take the edge off, and she prayed the alliance she'd started with Neal and the Mancusos would give her a way out of the life Mikhail had made for them.

"Why are we back at this place?" Katia asked. "It's so boring."

"Boring is underrated." Ana looked around. Sanctuary wasn't as busy as usual, but it was still quite full. Thankfully, since she wanted this next meeting with Neal to be somewhat clandestine. Mikhail was out of town for a few days which eliminated the possibility he might appear, but he had eyes everywhere and she couldn't be certain no one had followed them here. She'd considered going somewhere different, but a new venue was sure to raise more suspicion than revisiting this club that Mikhail didn't care for anyway. "I like it here. It's not as manic as the clubs Mikhail likes."

"True, true." Katia sipped her drink and glanced around the bar. "Are you meeting your new friend here or are we looking for someone, how shall I put this delicately, less rough around the edges?"

Ana heard the slight twinge of jealously, but she was used to Katia not wanting to share her with anyone. Still, she needed to get Katia under control if she was going to have any hope of carrying out her plans. "This is business, Katia. You forget that I am a custodian of my family's wealth as much as Mikhail is and I'm less likely to be distracted by material things and good-looking women." She stared hard into Katia's eyes, hoping she got the message. "If I choose to pursue personal interests, I will not let them interfere with business. Neal is a business arrangement. Nothing more. Do you understand?"

Katia's jaw clenched, but she nodded her assent, and Ana didn't push. Katia was a friend, but she too was a business arrangement, a gift from her father for not pushing back on the marriage to Mikhail. On some level, Katia must know she wouldn't have come to the States but for Ana's unique situation. If her union with Mikhail were to fall apart, would she still have a place here?

This was not the time to think of such things. She needed to be focused for her meeting with Neal.

Like she'd been conjured from thought, Neal appeared across the room, striding toward her, her eyes never straying from hers no matter how many people crossed her path on the way over. Ana lost complete track of time and a moment or an hour later, Neal appeared at her side. She held out her hand, and Ana looked down at it for a moment before she realized Neal was gesturing to her drink. She handed it over and watched while Neal slowly tipped the glass to her lips and took a long, slow swallow. Her eyes closed as she drank, like she was immersed in the experience, giving it her sole focus, and in that instant, Ana wished Neal was immersed in her as well.

"Thank you," Neal said as she handed her the now empty glass.

Ana shook away her decidedly unbusinesslike thoughts. "One would think you hadn't had a drink in days. Isn't liquor the heart of the Mancuso trade?"

Neal half-smiled. "Ironic, right? It seems someone delivered an entire truckload of liquor to our warehouse, but the bottles had been tampered with and they were empty. Can you believe that?"

"It sounds like your business isn't doing very well."

Both Ana and Neal turned toward Katia. Ana wanted to scold her, but also didn't want to give the impression in front of Neal that anything Katia said deserved much credence. While she cast about for the right approach, Neal beat her to it.

"Business is great, actually. We were already overstocked, so we didn't need the new shipment. We always seem to make things work. No matter who tries to interfere."

Ana bristled inwardly at the words, but she kept her steely mask in place. It was time to talk to Neal alone and she no longer cared about Katia's reaction. "That's great news. Now, I would like to talk to you about the arrangement we discussed. There are quiet rooms upstairs. Follow me." She took two steps before turning back to Katia. "Thank you for keeping an eye out. I couldn't do anything without you."

The words made her gag, but Katia's eyes softened at the praise and she knew she'd bought a bit of favor, hopefully enough to get Neal on board.

When they reached the last room off the hallway upstairs, Ana reached for the chain around her neck and slipped off a small key. She'd leased the private room in Mikhail's name months ago, but he didn't even know it existed. She'd used it for her assignations, but this was the first time for business. When she led Neal into the room, she glanced around looking for signs of past visits that might betray her, but everything was in its place. The bed was made, the desk was clear, and the bookshelves were full of rows of classics, designed to conceal any hint of controversy. This was her sanctuary.

"This is a beautiful space," Neal said. "It's all yours, right?"

"It is." She waited a few beats and then added, "I sometimes need a place to be alone."

Neal shot a look at the large king-sized bed with the canopy. "Alone?"

"I didn't bring you up here to discuss my personal life."

Neal shoved her hands in her pockets. "You're the one who brought me to your private place."

She was right, of course. Ana decided her primary goal needed to be keeping a level head while Neal was around or she wasn't going to accomplish much else. She pointed at two chairs in the corner of the room, far from the bed. "Let's sit. We have much to discuss."

Neal hesitated for a moment before following her across the room. She sat first, choosing the chair with the best view of the door, exactly as a bodyguard would.

"Do you like protecting people?" Ana let the question spill out despite the fact it was completely off topic. "Or is it simply a good way to make money?"

Neal cocked her head and drew in her bottom lip, a move Ana was starting to recognize as her thinking face. Silence followed for a few weighty moments before Neal finally spoke.

"It was never a job. Let's just say I was called to serve."

Ana waited for more, but Neal didn't add to the statement, leaving Ana to either conjure a follow-up question or fill in the blanks on her own. She'd done all the research she could do without drawing attention. Neal had been a college basketball star on a full scholarship to Tulane, certain to go on to stardom with the WNBA, but in her junior year, her world came crashing down. An injury took her out of the game forever. She dropped out of school and moved to Dallas where she started working for the Mancuso family. The internet trail dried up there, but the timing was too convenient to be a coincidence.

"And now you're in charge," Ana said, hoping to draw some sort of reaction. "Do you like it?"

"Who said I'm in charge?"

"You appear to be."

Neal's eyes took on a faraway look and Ana wanted to ask her what thoughts triggered the distraction, but the moment she'd observed felt a little personal to intrude upon.

After a moment, Neal squared her jaw and her voice was forceful like she was convincing herself as much as making a declaration. "Yes, I'm in charge."

Ana nodded. "Then that's settled, but you never answered my question."

"What question was that?"

"Do you like protecting people?"

"It's not what I do anymore."

Ana noted a somewhat wistful tone behind Neal's words. "Of course it is. When you fight for something as hard as you fought to win at Tulane, it creates a connection, a responsibility. When you're in charge, that obligation multiples."

Neal cocked her head. "How would you know?"

"You think I'm nothing more than a trophy wife, meddling in my husband's business."

"I didn't say that."

"You didn't have to. Something is causing you to hesitate when it comes to working with me." She waved her hands in a sweeping motion. "Until we clear the air, there is no sense moving forward."

Neal stood and leaned deep into her space. "The only one who can clear the air is you, and until you tell me exactly what you're up to, there's nothing more to discuss." She rocked back on her heels and her smile was broad and self-satisfied. "How's that for being in charge?"

❖

The silence between them was loud with portent, but with each passing second, Neal wondered if she'd pushed too hard and Ana would walk away. The rebellious part of her wanted to tell Ana to take her money and go, but the sensible part knew there'd be hell to pay if she blew this opportunity, no matter how sketchy it might seem. She'd watched Siobhan negotiate with enemies on behalf of the family so many times and she dug deep to find an appropriate response from her mentor's past accomplishments.

Get more than you give, but always let them think they bested you.

"The money is not enough. How do I know it's not traceable? How do I know that Mikhail isn't going to come looking for it, stoking a bigger fight? You say that he's working with Dominique but offer nothing to prove why she would betray her own family by aligning herself with their sworn enemy, and on top of that, you're asking me to essentially do the same by joining forces with you. The very least you can offer is a motive for your actions. Money means nothing if it comes with disaster."

Neal waited, poised and ready to head to the door, but hoping Ana would give her something, anything because as much as she feared the consequences of this alliance, she feared more what would happen if she was left without Ana's resources.

Ana settled onto the couch and pointed at the spot next to her. "Sit." After Neal didn't move, she softened her tone. "Please."

Neal took her time walking over to the couch and when she sat, she made sure she was as far from Ana as possible. Ana's very presence was incredibly distracting, and she didn't need anything to detract from her sole purpose. Siobhan had spent years under tight control, never letting the lure of beautiful women sway her from her focus on the family business. She'd come to clubs like Sanctuary, and partake in temporary pleasure, but relationships were relegated to business only.

Until she'd met Royal, and then her singular resolve had dissolved and she let passion lead her into a relationship with a sworn enemy of the family, an undercover FBI agent bent on bringing the entire family down. Now Siobhan had fled the country with the enemy and left their entire business in disarray, proving passion led to nothing good. She wasn't about to make the same mistake.

She shifted in her seat to face Ana, while still staying as far away as possible. "I'm waiting."

"I know." Ana sighed. "I told you before, my marriage to Mikhail was arranged when I was young. Before I knew who I really was or had a chance to plot out a future for myself. You cannot understand what it's like to grow up in Russia where everything is tightly controlled, and when you are a woman, even a rich woman from a prominent family, your choices are few."

Neal flashed to the picture that had hung in the living room of her childhood home of her mother and father standing before an altar, her mother's puffy dress barely covering the bump in her abdomen with yards of cheap tulle. Her father had lasted until two months after she'd been born before he controlled the situation by fleeing from it. "Don't tell me what I cannot understand."

Ana nodded. "My apologies. I do not know every detail of your past, but I do know you are able to go to clubs and pick up women without fear of reprisal."

"Is that what this is about? You want the freedom to pick up women? With the money you sent to us, you could buy any access you want."

"You underestimate me. Yes, I can buy whatever I want or need, except for the one thing I value most of all. My freedom. I will always be tied to Mikhail and his decisions, even if I have no control over the choices he makes. I can purchase comfort, but unless I can escape, I will never know freedom. That's where you come in."

Neal was curious, but leery. "You want me to help you divorce Mikhail?"

"There's no such thing as divorce in my world. Besides, paperwork is a minor distraction, Mikhail would never let me go. I need a more permanent solution."

Holy shit. Neal took a moment to reflect on the implications of killing Mikhail Petrov. His death or even an attempt on his life would spark an all-out war between their factions and, if Dominique really was working with Petrov, the Mancusos would not survive. Still, she had to be sure she understood what Ana was asking before she considered outright rejection. "You want me to kill Mikhail for you?"

Ana fixed her with an icy stare. "If there's killing to be done, I'm perfectly capable of making the arrangements. It's what happens after that needs to be carefully planned and executed."

She emphasized the word "executed" and Neal took note not to get on her shit list. Ana Petrov was a force and she was drawn to her in ways that could bring them all down. Was this how Siobhan had felt when she started to fall for Royal? While she kind of trusted Siobhan knew what she was doing with Royal, her continued absence and its effect on the family was taking a toll. She would not make the same mistake as her mentor in falling for her enemy, but she and Ana had the same goal when it came to Mikhail. If she was careful to guard her feelings, this might be the perfect arrangement.

"You'll have to tell me everything. I assume you want to disappear, or are you intending to take over?"

"I haven't decided." Ana reached out a hand and placed it on her knee. "Let's explore both options, shall we?"

The warmth of her hand seared through Neal, and she wanted to run, but she stayed in place hoping Ana didn't notice her discomfort or, if she did, didn't detect the source of it. "I have the connections you need to disappear, but if you intend to assume the business, that will be much more involved."

"But you can make it happen."

She wasn't sure, but she wasn't about to convey her lack of surety to Ana. It wasn't good business, but more than that, she wanted to do this thing for her. Mikhail was an ass, and anyone would want to break free, but it was more than that. Helping Ana dispose of him and take over the Petrov empire would bring her pleasure, and when it came to Ana, pleasure was something she definitely wanted to pursue.

"I need time, but yes, I can do this." She rattled off a list of information she needed from Ana. Proprietary information about the Petrov business, accounts, etc. She wasn't sure what all she would need so she mimicked the requests she'd heard Siobhan make in the past, trusting in her own ability to either figure out what to do next or find someone who could.

"Get this to me within two days," Neal said. "We have to move fast because if anyone knows you were here, meeting with me, then they will be on to you." She jerked her chin to the door. "What about your lady-in-waiting?"

"Katia?" Ana shook her head. "She's harmless."

"No one is harmless." Neal reached over and unbuttoned the first few buttons of Ana's blouse before reaching up and ruffling her hair. The faux flirtation was enough to send a surge of heat through her, and she very nearly leaned in to press her lips to Ana's before pulling back.

"What are you doing?" Ana asked, her voice a breathless whisper.

"Setting the stage." Neal pointed to the door. "A hundred dollars says she's right outside. Go first and let her see you like this and she'll think this meeting was nothing more than sex." She paused long enough to let the idea spark in the air. "You need to make her believe it."

Ana stood and very deliberately undid another button, revealing ample, ivory cleavage. Her hand lingered on her blouse while her eyes locked with Neal's and it was all Neal could do to remain upright. Next, Ana reached her free hand up along her neck, pulling her hair up and then shaking it loose in a sexy display of femininity that weakened Neal's knees. This woman was hot and dangerous, and she was going to be in big trouble if she stayed in this room another moment.

"Change of plans," she said. "I'm heading out. Stay here. If she comes looking for you, let her find you on the bed." She took two steps to the door and turned back. "Contact me when you have the information we'll need. And, Ana?"

"Yes, Neal?"

She started to say that next time they'd need to meet somewhere more formal, less likely to have a bed in the room, but the idea only conjured a vision of Ana with her blouse unbuttoned, lying on the bed, waiting for her, and the image robbed her of words. She shook her head. "Never mind."

The cold night air took the edge off as she left Sanctuary. She stopped on the street, torn between going home to process what had just happened and finding another club, another way to release the pent-up tension. She decided to walk for a bit and then choose, but she'd barely made it down the street when she spotted a tall shadow coming up close from behind and her senses went on high alert. When the figure drew closer, she turned swiftly and nearly collided with whoever it was.

Something that felt like hard metal pushed against her side and she looked down to see a gun protruding from the stranger's hand. Was this one of Mikhail's men, watching out for his wife while he was away?

"Don't speak."

The voice was slightly muffled through the scarf that covered the stranger's face, but it sounded vaguely familiar. Ignoring the gun in her side, she reached up and pushed aside the scarf, and the light from the nearby streetlamp revealed the stranger's identity.

"Royal?"

Royal nodded and placed a finger over her lips. She pointed to an SUV parked several feet away and motioned for Neal to walk in front of her, but Neal didn't budge. "Lose the gun," she whispered.

"Lose the attitude." She gestured to the door of the SUV. "Get in now."

Neal stared at the door and back at Royal. Siobhan may have fallen for this woman, but Neal didn't believe a life-long federal agent would blow up an undercover investigation and chunk her entire career over a woman even if that woman was Siobhan Collins. She was certain Royal was more interested in Siobhan's connections than her beauty and smarts. Siobhan may have fallen under Royal's spell, but she wasn't about to get into a vehicle with a rogue federal agent who was holding her at gunpoint.

She stepped to the side and swung her leg toward Royal's, knocking it out from under her. Royal lost her balance, but she caught herself on the fender of the car and lunged toward Neal who jumped backward out of her grasp. Royal lost hold of the gun in the process and it skittered across the pavement. Both of them dove for it and were rolling around on the pavement when a voice called out from the SUV.

"Stop that nonsense and get in the car. Both of you."

Neal pushed Royal off of her and looked toward the window of the SUV. The woman who'd spoken was in the shadows, but her brisk, no-nonsense tone was unmistakable.

Siobhan Collins had returned and now everything was about to change.

CHAPTER NINE

A na stood in her dressing room, staring in the mirror at her third choice of dresses for the evening. There was nothing wrong with any of the gowns she'd tried on so far, but none of them seemed special enough for her first foray back into Dallas society since the averted bombing at the museum benefit she'd attended over a month ago.

You're acting like a silly schoolgirl. No one is going to talk to you, socialize with you no matter what you wear.

It was true. Her connection to Mikhail made her a pariah at these events which meant she usually shied away from attending. She didn't get the hypocrisy that allowed the museum to gratefully accept the generous donations of the Mancuso family, only to act like her gift of three times that amount were tainted funds. Mikhail made fun of her for trying to fit in, but then again he'd never had any class and didn't care for anyone who did. One of the many reasons they'd never got along.

She reached for the Dior. She'd only worn it once before and the shimmery flow of the midnight blue gown had left a trail of breathless admirers. The other patrons might not talk to her or socialize with her, but they wouldn't be able to avoid looking at her and she could live with that small consolation.

Tonight's benefit was for the opera, and she'd taken advantage of the fact Mikhail was still out of town to arrange for a car service to take her to the bright red hall on the edge of downtown, not wanting one of Mikhail's henchmen to escort her to the event since he'd either scare the other patrons or report her every action to Mikhail. Or both.

Not that she had anything nefarious planned for the evening, but the idea of being monitored would rob the night of pleasure, and she needed a little pleasure right now. Her mind still whirred with the memory of Neal in her private room at Sanctuary. There'd been that moment when they'd almost kissed and the heat of the encounter seared them both. She hadn't imagined that. Or had she?

Damn. Now was not the time to start mistrusting her instincts. Her relationship with Neal was strictly business. It had to be or her plans wouldn't work. And they had to work because she couldn't stand to think the rest of her life would be nothing more than watching Mikhail indulge his every pleasure at her expense.

She managed to avoid any staff on her way downstairs, and she breathed a sigh of relief that Katia didn't show up as she often did when Mikhail was out of town. The driver was waiting by the servant entrance as she'd requested and he didn't bother her with small talk on the way downtown, which set a good tone for the rest of the evening. But when he started to pull up in front of the Winspear, she interrupted the silence. "Let's go around the building. It's a beautiful night and I'd like to see the park."

He shot her a curious look in the rearview mirror but proceeded to steer the car away from the many others queued up for the valet stand and drove around to the back of the building which faced the large park that covered the thoroughfare running through downtown. She didn't blame him for questioning her choice. In tall heels and a long gown, traipsing around wasn't ideal, but it would save her from the photographers gathered at the entrance to the opera hall, hoping to catch celebrity sightings. All she needed was Mikhail seeing her photo in the paper, accusing her of trying to step out on him, show him up by participating in society events he considered a waste of time and beneath him.

But she'd left a rich life, full of friends and functions, to fulfill the bargain her family had made to keep their fortunes going, and she'd be damned if he robbed her of this too. Generous donations bought her entrance to events like this one where she could at least pretend to be someone other than the wife of a mobster even if it was only for an evening at a time.

She made her way around the building and entered through one of the side doors. Waiters walked through the lobby, carrying trays of drinks and she took the first one offered, forcing herself to sip slowly. The opera tonight was *Carmen*, and she planned to stay for the entire three-hour production—a perfect way to avoid her cavernous, empty home and the life she'd grown to despise.

"Crab puff pastry?"

She looked up at the server, holding his tray toward her. She started to decline, but the morsels looked heavenly, and she'd skipped dinner. If she didn't eat something the champagne was going to go right to her head. She reached for a napkin and scooped up one of the bite-sized puffs.

"You should take more than one," the waiter said. "They're really good."

She bit into the one in her hand and nearly moaned with pleasure. He was right and she obliged by taking another. He moved on and she watched him go, half wishing she could steal his tray full of goodness, call the car service, and curl up in her suite at home with a bottle of Dom and these snacks. Maybe being alone wasn't so bad.

The moment the thought appeared so did a familiar face from across the room, and Ana sucked in a breath. Neal was wearing a tuxedo which was show-stopping enough, but with her towering height she outshone everyone else in the room. She stood completely still as if any movement might cause Neal to disappear like she'd been nothing more than an apparition, but when Neal's eyes met hers and she smiled, Ana knew her worries were misplaced.

But then another figure appeared beside her and Ana's mood went dark. Siobhan Collins was back and she wasn't smiling. What would that mean for her arrangement with Neal? If Siobhan was back to assume control of the Mancuso business, was Neal about to be relegated back to the role of bodyguard? Would she have any say about how things were managed, or was her moment of being in charge over for good?

Ana suspected the latter would be true. She tore her gaze from Neal and grabbed another glass of champagne from a passing waiter. She should find her seat, but it would look odd to leave the reception before the executive director for the opera had a chance to give his spiel to try to talk them all into opening their checkbooks and offering generous donations. If she wanted to fit in, she'd stay put. Her brain commenced a tiny tug-of-war between want and need and making something harder than it had to be. She wasn't very far into it when Neal started walking toward her, flanked by Siobhan and another woman who looked slightly familiar. This was not how she'd planned to see Neal again, but she had a feeling all her well-laid plans were about to unravel. She tipped the glass of champagne to finish it off, set it down on one of the tables scattered throughout the room, and fortified herself to meet her rivals, because no matter what arrangement she'd worked out with Neal, ultimately, they were adversaries, and she'd do well to remember it.

Neal pulled the sedan up to the valet stand at the Winspear and turned back to her two passengers, Siobhan and Royal, who were deep in the middle of a whispered conversation. "We're here."

Siobhan met her eyes and motioned to the building. "Guess this is as good a time as any to make a grand reentry. Let's go. Both of you."

Neal could see Royal hesitate and she could hardly blame her since no doubt the FBI was on the lookout for her since she'd abandoned her job to flee the country with Siobhan. For her own part, she didn't get why Siobhan insisted that she'd don a tux and show up for this or any event where the entire elite of Dallas society would show up to see and be seen. She'd accompanied Siobhan to plenty of functions, but she'd spent her time on the fringes, not mixing and mingling. She had absolutely nothing in common with any of these people which didn't bode well for fitting in.

"I'd like to go on record again that this seems like a bad idea," she said. "I don't have a clue what to say to any of these people, and Royal here is very likely to be arrested by the end of the night."

Siobhan rolled her eyes, leading Neal to believe Royal had raised exactly the same point. "You're perfectly capable of making small talk, which is all most of this crowd can manage, and Royal is not going to be arrested, although it's refreshing to see you care so much about her fate. Royal didn't do anything wrong other than quit her job. If they come after her, she's going to become a high-profile whistleblower and I'll have her booked on every major network to tell her story by tomorrow morning." She gave them both a hard stare. "I'm tired of being in hiding, and I'm not going to live in fear of what may happen. Don Carlo was a major sponsor of this event and I'm here to represent him as his daughter, and I want you both with me. Is that clear?"

Neal shot a look at Royal, the only one of them who had a choice in the matter, but Royal merely shrugged like the decision was completely out of her hands.

"Okay, I'm in." Neal left the keys in the ignition and stepped out of the car. She took the card from the valet and shoved it in her pocket. She started toward Siobhan's door, but one of the valets already had it open and had extended a hand to help her out of the car. Another demonstration of why her presence here wasn't necessary. With Siobhan and Royal back in town, she had no role in the family, and she'd been waiting since last night for the news her assistance was no longer necessary. But so far, all she'd gotten was a ride home from the club and a request, make that demand, to pick them both up for tonight's event. Oh, and a direct order to wear a tuxedo, which had been the most dreaded part of her day since finding a tux that fit her tall frame on short notice had been a challenge at best.

The lobby was packed with well-dressed patrons, and Neal stepped to the side of the crowd to size up the room. There were metal detectors at the entrances to the auditorium, but not at the main doors. She quickly spotted a few undercover cops or private security—hard to tell which—who circled through the crowd, constantly on alert. She looked over at Royal who was following her line of sight and gave her a subtle nod. She might not trust Royal, but she begrudgingly admitted she would rather have someone with her instincts as a friend instead of an enemy.

She followed Royal's gaze to see Siobhan snag three glasses of champagne from a passing waiter. She held them in one hand and slid her other around Royal's waist and led her over to where Neal was standing.

"Here," Siobhan said as she handed over one of the flutes. "You look like you could use a drink."

Neal took the glass, but only managed a sip before she spotted Ana standing across the room. She choked on the drink and set it on a nearby tray.

"What is it?" Siobhan asked, turning toward Ana.

"Don't look," Neal croaked. She cleared her throat. "Ana Petrov is here. What is she doing here?" The rhetorical question was meant to be silent, but she'd lost control at the sight of Ana in another devastatingly gorgeous dress. Another piece of vintage couture? Probably.

"Did you tell her you were coming tonight?" Siobhan asked.

"What are you talking about?"

"You think I don't know that you were in her private suite at the club last night?" Siobhan sighed. "You of all people should know better than to underestimate me. It wasn't a coincidence that we were exactly where you needed us to be when you stumbled out of Anastasia's room."

Neal's gut clenched. "You followed me."

"Not for the reason you think, but yes, we did."

"How long have you been back?"

"Not long. I was trying to find you to discuss business, but you were engaged in other pursuits."

Neal paused for a moment to consider her next words. She didn't like the idea Siobhan and Royal had been spying on her like she couldn't be trusted. They were the ones who'd left the country and left the family business in disarray while they were God knows where. She'd been tasked with keeping things together and she'd been doing the best she could in the wake of Don Carlo's death, Dominique's betrayal, and Siobhan's abdication. All she'd done in their absence was with a singular purpose—keep the family business together until Siobhan returned, but now she was back and everything, including the bond she'd had with Siobhan for all these years, seemed to be unraveling.

"We have a business arrangement. In case you missed it, we have a bit of a cash flow problem since Dominique took off with most of the family funds. Ana came to me with a proposition, and I accepted. You were gone and you haven't bothered to communicate other than cryptic messages from your old law school buddy, and I had to make a judgment call. But now you're back and you can do what you want, and clearly it's time for me to move on." She glared at Royal to punctuate her message and took a step toward the door.

"Wait."

She didn't turn back, but she didn't keep walking either, more curious about what Siobhan would have to say than anxious to get away from this place and these people. She didn't have to wait long.

"I put you in charge."

Siobhan's declaration was half accusation and plea. Neal needed to see her face to judge which. She turned and faced her employer. "But you're here now, so it's back to you." She touched her hand to her forehead in a mock salute. "If it's okay with you, I'll simply slip back into the shadows."

She started to walk away again, but this time Siobhan grabbed her arm and stepped into her space.

"It's not okay," Siobhan said. "I can't do this on my own. I need you. I need Michael. We're the inner circle. We're the only circle now."

Neal glanced over at Royal who was trying to pretend like she wasn't listening to every word.

"Yes, her too," Siobhan said, reading her mind. "If you trust me, you have to trust her too."

She didn't like it, but it wasn't up to her. She could walk away right now. She had money saved. She could go back to New Orleans, find a place near her sister. It had been years, and it wasn't likely anyone there would remember her or care any longer about exacting revenge. But what would she do? Her work as a bodyguard for a crime family didn't easily translate into a position in the outside world. It wasn't like she had a résumé and references.

"I do trust you, but you don't need a bodyguard anymore." She shot another pointed look at Royal.

"You're right. I don't need a bodyguard. But I do need a capo I can trust. I am the firstborn child of Don Carlo and Don Carlo has died. Your Don is asking you to serve. What say you?"

The room was teeming with people, staff and guests, all milling around, networking, socializing, eating and drinking, and the buzz of the crowd was a constant hum. The numbing noise was the perfect backdrop to the whirlwind of emotion Neal felt in that moment. She'd never considered becoming a made member of the Mancuso family. She'd been hired for her size, her desperation, and her debt. She'd been nothing but loyal since the day Don Carlo had saved her life, but her reward had been granted long ago and she'd been paid in full.

But now Siobhan, the true heir to the family business was standing in front of her, offering her a life of not only security, but opportunity. Being temporarily in charge was one thing, but being made meant she'd be protected instead of always being the one doing the protection. She'd never want for anything, and she'd always share in the spoils. There was only one answer to Siobhan's question, no matter what it meant for her future and the deal she'd made with Ana. "Yes. I'm at your service. I always have been."

"I know." Siobhan looked around. "I promise we'll do this more formally later. Tonight is about reconnaissance. You need to use your connection to Ana Petrov to find out what's going on with Mikhail and Dominique. You're right—they are working together, but Dominique is staying out of sight, and we need to flush her out. If you can get Ana to divulge what she knows, we might have a chance."

Neal nodded, but the promise she'd already made to Ana burned in the back of her mind. "And what about what Ana wants?"

"Ana Petrov may act like her motives are pure, but she married Mikhail, which already calls her judgment into question. Whatever she's told you she wants from you, you can bet there will be strings attached. You should continue to act like you're going to fulfill your end of any bargain you've made, but tread carefully. She's trouble."

It was a reasonable warning, but Neal's first instinct was to protest. To tell Siobhan that Ana wasn't like that, but she quickly realized she didn't know that was true. She didn't know Ana at all other than she'd said she would help and she'd fulfilled that promise by sending cash. Lots of it. A worthy demonstration of her commitment. Surely, that was something. Right?

"Let's go talk to her," Neal said. "All three of us."

"It might be a good idea," Royal said, the first words she'd spoken in moments. "The bureau knows almost nothing about her, only her family, and I doubt any agents have had any interaction with her. This is the perfect opportunity to get a jump on the situation. Neal can do most of the talking while we size her up."

"Fine," Siobhan said. "Let's go, but I'm not going to be late for the seating."

Neal led the way through the crowded reception, her eyes fixed on Ana's the entire way. Ana looked calm and collected, but Neal caught a slight undercurrent of worry in her glances at Siobhan and Royal and it occurred to her that Ana might try to use Royal's status as a fugitive for leverage. When they reached Ana's side, Neal leaned in to whisper, "If you make a fuss, it will be the end of our arrangement."

"Do I look like the kind of woman that makes fusses?"

Neal smiled, as much for show as because she was amused by Ana's feisty response. "Anastasia Petrov, I'd like you to meet my friends Siobhan and Royal."

Ana matched Neal's smile and held out her hand. "My pleasure. I'm glad you could both make it this evening. I understand you've been traveling."

"A necessary duty," Siobhan said, clasping Ana's hand. "And I understand you'd like to have the opportunity to travel as well. Or was it that you'd prefer your husband take a permanent vacation, a wish I'm sure we all share?"

Ana raised her eyebrows ever so slightly in Neal's direction and Neal lifted her shoulders in response. There wasn't anything she could do about Siobhan's comment. Did Ana really think she'd keep secrets from her boss now that Siobhan was back in town?

"My husband has his own life, Siobhan," Ana said. "But neither one of us has fallen prey to the charms of a federal agent. Do you make a habit of living on the edge or has the death of your Don robbed you of your good sense?"

Shit. Neal instinctively stepped closer to Siobhan as if to protect her from Ana's cutting words, but when she spotted Royal doing the same, she realized she might be the one who needed protecting for attempting to bring Ana into the fold. She glared at Ana who didn't appear to be fazed at the exchange.

"You have a funny way of making friends," Siobhan said. "Maybe you should—"

Her words were cut short by loud laughter coming from behind her. Neal turned to find Mikhail Petrov on her heels. Double shit.

"Are these people bothering you, Anastasia?" he bellowed.

❖

Ana held in a gasp while Mikhail beckoned to a hulking figure standing nearby. "You would like me to have them escorted out, yes?"

Ana's mind whirred with questions. How had Mikhail found her this evening and how had he gotten into this ticket-only event? Her suspicions about the former centered on Katia, but it could just as easily have been one of the servants Mikhail paid to spy on her. Still, when she got home, Katia was going to get a grilling. In the meantime, she forced a smile. "Well, hello, Mikhail. I'm so glad to see you made it back early from your trip. Unfortunately, I only have one ticket for tonight's show."

"Show? We're not staying for this. No one in this country can do justice to the greats." He punctuated his disdain with a rough grab of her arm. She wanted to push him off of her, but she wanted to exit gracefully with her pride intact more, so she smiled indulgently at her boorish husband. "You're such a nationalist, Mikhail. Don't you know that's no longer in fashion?"

His eyes widened and his jaw set. He might be boorish, but he wasn't stupid. She needed to get him out of here before he realized she was making fun of him in front of the Mancuso contingent. She placed a hand on the arm holding hers, squeezed gently, and prayed Neal could tell she was doing this for show. "But now that you're home, I think we should go. We have some catching up to do."

His frown softened and he grunted and motioned for her to follow him, but when he turned to go, Neal stepped into his space. "Move, bitch," he growled.

"Ana, you don't have to go."

"'Ana, you don't have to go'," Mikhail mimicked her with a high-pitch, singsong voice. He laughed and pointed at Neal. "Your new friend is pining for you already, but this one is too tall, too coarse for you." He looked around the room. "There are many beautiful women here if you want to indulge your guilty pleasures. Women I would much rather watch kiss my wife than this loser."

Ana could see the fury redden Neal's face, and she silently willed her not to act on her anger. This wasn't the time or place, and a public fight would only come back to bite her if and when Mikhail ever met his fate. Siobhan put a hand on Neal's arm and gave her a nod. That's right, Siobhan was a lawyer. She understood the predicament. Ana wanted to stay for the opera, but leaving with Mikhail now was her only choice if she wanted a future without him someday. Protecting Neal was a bonus.

She laced her fingers through Mikhail's and tugged him closer. "Let's go."

She saw the self-satisfied grin he gave to Neal and her friends, but she couldn't bear to look at them herself to see their reaction. She might have lost this battle, but she was here to win the war. Hopefully, Neal understood, but if she didn't there wasn't much she could do about it, and the thought filled her with regret.

CHAPTER TEN

Neal sat in one of the chairs opposite Don Carlo's desk and Royal sat in the other. Michael stood by the door to the study and held it open as Siobhan walked through. She glided past them and slipped into the high-backed chair behind the desk like she belonged in the seat of power.

And she did.

"We have to make some changes," Siobhan said.

"That's pretty broad," Neal said. "Care to be more specific?"

"We need to keep everything aboveboard until things die down, and legitimate liquor sales aren't going to get us where we need to be. We either need to pivot or supplement until we can find Dominque and get her to cough up everything we need to know about the funds she stole."

"What about the money from Ana?" Neal asked. "Are we acting like that never happened?"

"It's a last resort. Those funds come with conditions, the details of which we're not completely aware. We're not desperate enough to strike a deal like that. Not yet anyway."

"Something's been bothering me," Royal said. "Ana Petrov looked very familiar to me."

"Probably because your fed buddies have shown you a million pictures of their most-wanted list," Neal said.

Royal shook her head. "Not even. I've never seen a photo of Ana Petrov. I always assumed it was because she was camera shy, but it may be that she's simply more clever than the rest of us and stayed out of the path of cameras on purpose. Maybe it's my imagination, but everything about the night felt familiar." Her eyes widened. "Wait a minute." She pulled out her phone and started scrolling.

"What is it?" Siobhan asked.

Royal held up a hand. "Hang on just one second." She kept scrolling. "Here we go." She held out her phone so both Neal and Siobhan could see. "She was at the museum the night of the bomb threat."

Neal held out her hand. "Let me see." She took the phone from Royal and blew up the photo. Sure enough, there was Ana standing alone with a champagne flute in her hand. Her dress was different, but otherwise, it was almost an exact replica of the scene from this past Saturday night. "Yeah, that's her, but so what? She attends social functions. Is that really such a big deal?"

"I'll tell you why," Royal said. "She hardly ever appears in public, not where cameras are around, but here she is at a benefit where a bomb threat cleared the entire museum, and she was at the opera for another benefit this weekend. Both of those events had one thing in common."

Siobhan's presence was the common theme. Neal's palms grew sweaty, and a chill ran down her spine as she absorbed the silent judgment behind Royal's words. She was the bodyguard and twice now her charge had been in the path of danger, and she'd done nothing to protect her. Hell, she hadn't even been aware of the threat. "It wasn't my decision to stay behind the night of the museum benefit."

"She's right, Royal," Siobhan said. "I ditched her to spend the evening with you."

"Fine, but if the Petrovs are trying to kill you, you'd think the people who were hired to protect you would have some intel about it."

Neal looked over at Michael, seeking an ally because Royal was essentially calling him out too, but he gave her a slight shake of his head. Was she really supposed to sit here and take Royal's trash talk without defending herself?

"I thought the police never found a bomb," she said. "Maybe the whole thing was a diversion. For all we know Ana could've been the target of whatever was going on."

"Or the mastermind," Royal said. "Mikhail may be fearless, but he isn't very smart. Someone with brains is running his operation."

She was right, but Neal couldn't imagine Ana being the ruthless mastermind behind the kind of shady dealings Mikhail was engaged in—prostitution, drugs, and God knows what else. Ana seemed too classy for such pursuits.

You don't know anything about her.

It was true, but she'd been in this business long enough to have learned how to read people and Ana's desperate plea for help shedding Mikhail from her life felt genuine, but what if her desperation was more about taking control of the Petrov empire and keeping it the way it was than a desire to be rid of a horrible husband? Was her attraction to Ana clouding her judgment?

"Neal, did you hear what I just said?"

She snapped to attention at Siobhan's voice. "Sorry, no."

"You're the best person to sort this out. She obviously trusts you, and I doubt she trusts many people. Get close to her and find out what you can. It's possible she's the one working with Dominique, not Mikhail. If that's the case, then they will both suffer the same fate."

She should be thrilled to get such a big assignment immediately after becoming made, but dread filled Neal at the prospect of taking Ana down with the rest of the Petrovs.

❖

Ana stood in her bedroom with her ear pressed against the door. Mikhail had been on a tear with the staff all morning, and she hoped the sudden silence meant he'd finally left to go to visit one of his many seedy brothels where he maintained backroom offices.

She eased open the door and gasped when she found Katia standing only inches away. "What are you doing here?"

Katia gave her a curious look. "We have a fitting at Francine's. Did you forget?"

She had. She'd forgotten everything since Saturday night's disaster at the opera, and she hadn't left her suite since the embarrassing foray. A dress fitting seemed like a silly way to end her self-imposed exile. "I can't go."

"You've been cooped up for days. Surely, you're feeling better by now."

"What?"

"Mikhail said you weren't feeling well. He asked me to stay away."

Leave it to him to make excuses for her absence that had nothing to do with the real reason she'd gone into seclusion, but she was relieved not to have to explain. Add to that she was still stewing because she was certain Katia was the one who'd told Mikhail where she was the night of the opera benefit. She considered confronting her but decided it would be more strategic to let Katia think she was still a trusted confidant. "I am better, but I'm not sure shopping is in the cards for me today."

"You have something better planned?"

She didn't, but not for lack of trying. She'd been thinking of ways to get a message to Neal, but no solutions had come to mind since she'd been under Mikhail's watchful eyes the past few days. Perhaps an outing would inspire some opportunity. She summoned fortitude she didn't feel, determined to find a way to make the trip downtown pay off. "Fine. I'll go."

Katia grinned. "Excellent. I already made reservations for tea at the Adolphus after. Go put on something fabulous and I'll meet you downstairs." She dashed off before Ana could protest an afternoon of mindless materialism followed by a decadent high tea, but maybe it was exactly what she needed to shake her malaise.

Fifteen minutes later, they were both in the back of a car chauffeured by one of Mikhail's men headed to Francine's. The small dress shop was known for catering to the wealthy elite of Dallas, but their inventory wasn't limited to dresses only. They also sourced other creature comforts designed to give their patrons the very best experience. She'd partaken in the past, but she wasn't in the mood for a tryst with a stranger today.

If Neal were here, you would indulge.

Totally different and no I wouldn't.

"Did you say something?" Katia asked.

"No." Ana bit her lip and banished those kinds of thoughts about Neal from her mind. Neal was a means to an end, and she couldn't let her become a distraction, but perhaps taking advantage of one of the private rooms might afford her an opportunity to get in touch with her. For business and no more. She touched the slim phone in her pocket, her fingers itching to send a text or make a call to reestablish their connection, but she shouldn't risk it until she knew she was completely alone, safe from the listening ears of the staff at the house or even Katia.

Francine, the owner, was on hand to greet them effusively. Ana wasn't impressed. Yes, she was a regular, but if she didn't spend lavishly, the woman would ignore her in favor of others who frequented her salon. No matter how much champagne she poured or private recreation she made available, Francine was all business and the perks were a means to an end. Ana respected her approach.

The dresses she'd ordered several weeks ago required little tailoring and her fitting was complete in less than thirty minutes. Katia, on the other hand, had a much harder time, and while she stood stock-still as the tailor jabbed her frocks with pins, Ana signaled to Francine she was interested in exploring something other than dresses. Francine complied by leading her to one of the private rooms.

She'd been in this room a few times and she favored the midnight blue furnishings and soft lighting. While she waited for her company, she pulled out the phone and sent a quick text to Neal.

Downtown. Adolphus. An hour.

An hour should be plenty of time for whatever was about to happen. She'd barely tucked away the phone when she heard a light knock on the door. "Come in."

She recognized Lauren from a past visit. Francine had likely assumed she'd want the comfort of a familiar face, and normally she'd be right, but in this moment, Ana wished a complete stranger had walked through the door. It would be easier then to explain she was more interested in company than sex.

"It's good to see you again."

"It's good to see you too."

Lauren stepped closer and ran a hand down her arm. "You're all dressed. I hoped to catch you in between outfits."

It wasn't next-level flirting, but it had done the trick in the past. But she'd felt more desperate in the past, like there was no way out and these backroom trysts were all that was available to her. Now, she was starting to see a way out and basic flirting and clandestine sex seemed like a waste of time and energy when she could be so close to having much, much more. She reached for Lauren's hand and removed it from her arm. "I need something different from you today."

Lauren gave her a pout, but she knew it wasn't real, a fact borne out when she reached into her bag and pulled out a stack of large bills. She dangled the money in front of Lauren and enjoyed the way she perked up in response.

"Whatever you need."

Ana described what she had in mind while Lauren nodded in response. It might not be the smartest move to trust a fit model/sex worker with her spying, but the circle of people she could trust grew smaller by the day. Everything about what she had planned involved taking chances, and in the scheme of things, it seemed low risk since Mikhail was unlikely to ever encounter one of the models at this little dress shop. Enough with the ruminations. It was time to act. "I need you to deliver a message."

❖

Neal's phone buzzed in her pocket, but her hands were too full to answer. She'd been working with the guys in the stockroom at Valentino's, relocating the liquor bottles Ana had sent over to a more secure location. A couple of them commented on how light the boxes were, but it was doubtful they suspected the specific reason why.

When the bottles were all stowed away, she reached for her phone to check her messages. The persistent caller hadn't left a voice message, but there was a text on the screen and though it was a different number than before, she instantly knew it was from Ana.

Downtown. Adolphus. An hour.

An hour? She checked the time now and the time of the text. She had thirty minutes if she wanted to make it on time. It would be tight, but she could do it. Her fingers hovered over the phone for a few minutes while she agonized about what to say, but finally she settled on the only answer that made sense. *See you there.*

She arrived at the hotel with ten minutes to spare, but with no street parking in sight, she reluctantly pulled up to the valet stand and handed over her keys. The bellman who opened the door for her didn't flinch at her dusty boots and rumpled shirt, probably because the SUV she was driving was worth more than he made in several years' salary, but she wished she'd taken a moment to change before charging over here since Ana would likely be decked out as usual.

Neal walked through the lobby, doing her best to act casual, while keeping a watchful eye for Ana to arrive, but after twenty minutes of loitering, she grew antsy. *Where are you?*

She fired off the text and almost immediately received a response.

Delayed. Wait for me?

Damn. Was Ana jerking her around? Short of hanging out at the bar she'd run out of ways to act like she belonged, and while a midday drink sounded like a good idea, she wanted to remain sharp. She walked back toward the door to the valet stand and scanned the few people checking in. No sign of Ana, but the one clerk at the front desk with no line gave her an idea.

"May I help you?" the woman asked.

Neal reached for her wallet. "Yes, I need a room."

"Excellent. How long will you be staying with us?"

She hesitated. "I'm not sure. Can we make it open-ended?"

The woman smiled. "Absolutely." She explained the cancellation policy and started typing on her computer. "I have a nice king room on the third floor or if you'd prefer, the terrace suite is available and it has a lovely view."

She listened to the woman give a full description of the suite. She only needed the room since the primary purpose of the booking was to give her a place to hang out until Ana arrived and to give them some privacy to talk on neutral ground. But the suite would be even more private, and a bold gesture designed to impress Ana. Besides it was the kind of indulgence she rarely let herself enjoy. "I'll take it." She pulled a fake ID and a stack of hundred-dollar bills from her wallet, inwardly smiling at the irony of paying for the room with some of the money Ana had delivered to Valentino's.

The suite was everything the woman had promised. She checked her phone again, but there was no new message from Ana. She typed in the room number and clicked send, then kicked off her boots and settled onto the couch. She should be out looking for Dominique or checking in with Michael who was doing the same, but she hadn't slept in days and the idea of a few minutes on the couch was too appealing to resist. She checked her phone one more time before she closed her eyes, but still no response from Ana. She'd give her an hour. She wasn't sure what would happen after that, but a few minutes of rest would hopefully give her a plan.

CHAPTER ELEVEN

Neal shot up at the noise, but it took her a moment to figure out someone was knocking on the door. Michael was the only one who showed up at her house unannounced, but he was supposed to be staking out Dominique's place today. She stumbled to the door, nearly tripping over a table before she found the light switch and realized she wasn't at home in her apartment.

The Adolphus. Right. She was supposed to meet Ana here. She checked her phone and quickly calculated it had been over an hour since she'd checked in. Damn, she must've fallen into a pretty deep sleep. She rubbed her eyes and looked out the door viewer to see a gorgeous woman standing in the hallway outside her room. She started not to answer, convinced the woman had the wrong room, but then she held up an envelope with her name scrawled on the front in a flowing script. She checked to make sure she had her key and stepped into the hallway. "Can I help you?"

"I'm Lauren. A mutual friend asked me to deliver this to you." She held out the envelope.

The woman looked vaguely familiar, but Neal couldn't place her. She stared at the envelope, curious about what was inside, but sensing danger as well. "Tell me her name."

"She asked me to be discreet."

Neal wasn't in the mood for this cloak-and-dagger shit. "Tell me her name or you can tell her you were unsuccessful in your mission."

Lauren sighed, looked around, and then leaned in close. "Anastasia Petrov."

"And how do you know her?"

"She comes to Francine's to shop. I met her there."

Ah, that explained why Lauren looked familiar. Siobhan frequented Francine's as well, and before she met Royal, she'd often partake of the private services the fit models provided to particular patrons. Was Lauren one of the models who offered the extra service, and if so, was that what had delayed Ana today? The idea of Ana being undressed by this beauty both turned her on and made her angry. How dare Ana ask her to wait while she played.

Like you weren't considering playing with her yourself. Why else did you get this suite if not to impress her?

She couldn't deny the truth of the thought, but it didn't make her feel less foolish. "Tell her I'm not interested." She pointed at the envelope, still in Lauren's hand. "And you can take that back to her."

"I can't actually. I made a promise to deliver this message and I keep my promises."

"How honorable." Neal stepped back into the suite and started to shut the door, but before it closed, Lauren reached a hand in and dropped the envelope to the floor. Neal watched it fall and when she looked back up, Lauren was halfway down the hall. She considered going after her but shut the door instead and stared at the cream colored envelope sitting on the floor. She bent to pick it up and pulled the card out of the envelope, but before she could read the contents another knock at the door drew her attention. She shoved the note into her pocket and swung open the door, certain she'd find Ana standing on the other side.

She was wrong.

"Hello, Neal. Nice suite. Did you spend my father's money to afford it?"

Dominique Mancuso was a striking figure on a normal day, but today she was wearing a charcoal gray power suit with wide legs and a jade green blouse. She didn't look like a woman who'd been on the run or full of grief over the loss of her father. No, she looked like a well-heeled boss, which was exactly what she would be if Don Carlo hadn't made his deathbed confession that Siobhan was his firstborn daughter. Neal chose her words carefully while she sized up the best way to play this encounter without letting Dominique know they were on to her.

"You know I'd never take a dime from your family I didn't earn."

"Is that a dig, Neal? I heard a rumor that your charge thinks I made off with the family fortune. Do you think I didn't earn it?"

She was being baited and she wasn't falling for it. Neal shrugged. "Not my fortune. Not my problem."

"Is that so? Last I checked, if Siobhan says jump, you say 'how high.'"

"Show's how little you pay attention. Siobhan isn't like you."

"I think it's cute the way you try and protect her reputation. Is that a bodyguard thing?"

"Is there something you want, Dominique?"

"Matter of fact there is. I could use your services. If you're finally over taking orders from Siobhan, come and work with me."

"What exactly are you doing? From what I can tell, the family business is defunct."

"The family has a new business. Come with me and I'll tell you all about it." She glanced at her watch. "But we have to leave right now. I have a car waiting downstairs."

This was insane. Her assignment was to stick to Ana and find out everything she knew. Sure, she was also supposed to be on the lookout for Dominique, but she hadn't expected to show up on her doorstep, especially when the doorstep wasn't even really hers. Which begged the question of how Dominique had found her in the first place. She didn't dare ask, but she vowed to figure it out.

Her hand strayed to the note in her pocket. What had Ana wanted to tell her that was so important, she risked having a model walk it over to her? Where was Ana and why hadn't she shown up for the meeting she insisted on?

"Are you coming?" Dominque asked, tapping her foot impatiently on the carpet.

"Yes." Neal surprised herself with the pronouncement, but she didn't see any way around it. She'd agreed to meet Ana in order to figure out the best way to find Dominique and now that motive didn't factor in. Besides, Ana had chosen to send a hooker with a note instead of bothering to show up herself. Decision made, Neal sidestepped Dominque and slid past her to exit her room. "You said you have a car waiting?"

❖

"You said she was there?" Ana paced outside of the French Room where Katia was already well into high tea. She'd received Lauren's text and told Katia she had to go to the ladies' room so she could hear what Lauren had to say in person.

"Yes," Lauren said. "She was there."

"But you did nothing."

"I wouldn't call it nothing. I gave her the note even though she refused to accept it. She practically ordered me to leave so I did, but I waited for a few minutes down the hall to see if she might change her mind, and that's when the others showed up."

Ana snapped to attention. "Others? What others?"

"A woman and two men. Your friend let the woman in, but the men stayed in the hallway."

Ana's brain was firing in a million different directions and growing more anxious with each thought. It had been two hours since she'd first texted Neal to ask her to meet her here at the hotel. Ostensibly, their rendezvous should be the only reason Neal was here at all, but she'd refused to even accept a note from her explaining why she was late and apparently, she'd had time to arrange a meeting with another woman. It didn't make sense. Something else had to be going on. "Describe the woman."

Lauren bit her lip like she was pondering. "Medium height. Pretty. No, make that striking. Long, dark hair and deep brown eyes. She looked a little familiar, but I can't place her."

It wouldn't pass for courtroom testimony, but it was something. Ana pulled out her phone and did a google search for an image. She shoved the phone in Lauren's direction. "Is this her?"

Lauren's eyes widened. "It is. Who is that?"

Ana stared at her, trying to discern if she really didn't know or if she had an ulterior motive for faking. She finally decided on the former. "Dominique Mancuso. Don't tell me you've never met her at Francine's."

"I haven't. I've met her sister, Celia, but never Dominique. If she frequents the shop, she must come in when I'm not there. I've heard stories about her though."

"I bet you have. What time did they leave?"

"Not ten minutes ago. They went down the freight elevator."

Ana glanced back at the French Room and contemplated her options. If she bailed on Katia without a decent explanation, there would be a price to pay, but if she stayed here, sipping tea and eating finger sandwiches while Neal was in trouble would she be able to live with herself?

She's not your problem.

No, but she might be my solution. "Go back to the shop. Do not speak of this. To anyone. Understood?"

Lauren nodded and backed away. Hopefully, the large sum Ana had given her earlier would purchase her silence but if not, she'd deal with Lauren another way. In the meantime, she needed to find Neal.

She made her way to the front desk, prepared to concoct a story designed to give her access to Neal's room, but once she mentioned the room number and her name, the clerk produced a key.

"She left instructions to provide you access. Do you need anything else, Ms. Petrov?"

Ana smiled at the assumption, took the key, and made her way to the suite. Once she was at the door, she knocked just in case Neal had returned, but after waiting a few minutes in the hall with no response, she slid the key in the lock and pushed her way inside.

The suite was empty, and aside for a melting bucket of ice on a tray with a bottle of Jameson's and two highball glasses, she'd have thought the front desk sent her to the wrong room. She walked around the large space, looking for some clue about where Neal may have gone, but she found nothing else except the envelope she'd given to Lauren to deliver, and it was empty. Had Neal read her note? If she had, surely, she would've stayed here and waited.

Unless the decision to leave hadn't been a choice at all. And that was the only explanation that made sense. She sat on the corner of the bed and attempted to untangle her jumbled thoughts. She would've expected Mikhail as the most likely candidate to abduct Neal. Not because he was jealous—she doubted he even gave her a second thought in that way since she'd reached her forties—but he likely suspected Neal knew things about the Mancuso family that would give him an advantage. Things even Dominique didn't know, which was exactly the reason Dominique had taken Neal. If she and Mikhail were working together, then access to someone in Siobhan's inner circle would all but guarantee Mancusos' demise.

She needed to get out of here and make a plan. She had compiled a list of all of Mikhail's holdings, even those he thought were a well-kept secret. She'd been preparing for years for the right time to break free, but if he managed to strengthen his position by taking over the Mancuso empire, she'd have to start over from the beginning.

That wasn't going to happen.

She poured two fingers from the whiskey bottle and took a deep draught. The amber gold with its layered complexity was far superior to the thin, flavorless vodka Mikhail preferred—the perfect metaphor for her life. She was done living life on the surface and ready to dive deep into substance, happiness. She must have control over her destiny.

She rode the elevator downstairs and took a moment to breathe before reentering the French Room where Katia was no doubt indulging her appetite for fancy food and wondering why she'd disappeared. Ana practiced a carefree smile, a breezy story about how she'd been distracted by the new fashion in the hotel boutique on her way back from the ladies' room and completely lost track of time, throwing in a self-deprecating remark about her flightiness. The script was easy to memorize since she'd been acting for years. But now every move she made was a means to an end, and she threw her entire being into pretending because deception would bring her closer to freedom. And nothing and no one, not Katia, not Mikhail, not Dominique, would stand in her way.

CHAPTER TWELVE

Neal ignored her phone the first time it buzzed, but the persistent texter was not going to be ignored.

"Go ahead and answer it," Dominique said. "You're not a prisoner here. You agreed to come with us willingly."

Right. It wasn't entirely clear she'd had an option, but it was true she'd agreed to accompany Dominique. Now, riding with her in the back of a plush limousine, complete with a full bar and a tray full of fancy snacks, anyone looking in would assume they were allies at least, but more likely friends. She was fine with the veneer because it would give her access, but she wasn't fooled about what was really happening here. Dominique wanted something and she would only be courted until she was no longer useful. She turned her phone over and folded her hands. "I'm good. Thanks."

Dominique handed her a glass. "You're a whiskey drinker, right?" She shuddered. "I figure you picked up that nasty habit from Siobhan." She leaned in uncomfortably close. "She thinks everyone should be like her, am I right?"

Neal *had* started drinking whiskey because of Siobhan, and she remembered fondly the first bottle of single malt scotch she'd received as a gift from her employer. It had been aged eighteen years and after tasting it, she swore she'd never go back to the rotgut liquor of her college days. She'd never admit any of this to Dominique, but her purpose here was to gain information, and one thing she'd learned from Siobhan was that sometimes you have to play a role to get what you wanted. "She does know what she likes, that's for sure."

Dominique squeezed her arm. "You're so diplomatic. Not what I expected. Of course, she never let you speak to us, so I had no idea what to expect."

Neal let the comment lie rather than point out that this was the very first time Dominique had ever treated her like anything other than a wall ornament. Better simply to change the subject. "Where are you taking me?"

Dominique's smile was feral. "To the future, Neal. To the future." She rapped on the glass and when the driver lowered it, she said. "We should be there by now. Step on it."

The car pulled to a stop a few minutes later, and Dominique's eyes brightened, and she clapped her hands. "Finally," she said. "Are you ready?"

Neal forced a smile. "I'm always ready for a new adventure."

"So full of surprises." The driver opened the door and Dominque stepped out. Neal stared at him for a moment, and he didn't flinch under the inspection. She'd half expected to recognize one of Mikhail's henchmen, but he didn't look familiar.

Dominique motioned for her to follow, and they walked down the sidewalk together. They were in Deep Ellum, not far from downtown. This area had been gentrified with shops, nightclubs, offices, and apartments, while keeping its warehouse district feel. Neal was surprised they were someplace so familiar. She'd expected something a little more cloak-and-dagger for the show Dominique was putting on.

"Where are we going?"

"It's a surprise." Dominique put a finger over her lips. "Don't worry. It'll be worth it." She stopped and rapped on a large metal door, marked only with the number 509. Seconds passed and Neal was beginning to think this excursion was a waste of time when the door eased open. Dominique pushed it the rest of the way and then beckoned for Neal to follow. She regretted handing over her gun, but no way was she going to back out now that she'd come this far. She stepped inside and looked around for the person who'd let them in, but they were all alone in the foyer of the building. The floor was marble tile and the walls were lined with the kind of wallpaper you'd find in your great-grandmother's house. She sniffed the air, half expecting a musty scent, but it smelled like fresh cedar.

"What is this place?" she asked.

"So impatient." Dominique grabbed her hand and led her down the hall. She stood in front of a bookcase and reached for a volume of Shakespeare. Like in an old movie, the shelf began to move, turning until it revealed a hidden passageway. Dominique pointed inside. "Isn't it charming?"

Neal nodded and followed her into the secret passageway. They walked about a hundred feet until they came to another door. Neal could hear noise now, conversation and music, but she couldn't make out any words. Dominique rapped on the door and it opened immediately. Neal instantly recognized the man who stood on the other side. It was Celia Mancuso's husband, Tony.

"What's she doing here?" he asked.

Dominique shoved her way past him. "I decide who enters and who leaves." She looked back at Neal. "Come on. We have work to do."

Neal faced Tony head-on as she walked by, determined to let him know he didn't intimidate her. Siobhan had always thought Celia married beneath her and he probably knew that and attributed whatever Siobhan thought to her as well. Fact was she didn't give a shit who Celia married. It wasn't her business and as long as Don Carlo had blessed the marriage that was all that mattered to her. But if Tony was here with Dominique, then Siobhan had been right about him not being worthy of joining the Mancuso family. Was Celia part of this enterprise as well?

"This is the new family business," Dominique said as if in answer to her silent question. "We're taking the best of what was and combining it with all of the things Daddy never let us do. Allow me to show you around."

A few turns in the room allowed Neal to take in enough—blackjack and poker tables and decked out bars in each corner—to realize she was in the middle of what was essentially a speakeasy and illegal casino. It wasn't like most of Don Carlo's businesses were legal, but they at least masqueraded as legitimate. This place wasn't even trying, and its eyes wide shut mystique only lent to the sketchy aura. "I think I get the idea."

"Trust me. The private rooms are spectacular."

Mildly curious about what constituted spectacular, Neal followed Dominique to a door on the far end of the great room. It opened into a hallway lined with more doors and Dominique selected the first one to the right. As she walked inside, the lights came on, dim, but enough to illuminate the features inside. A large four-poster bed was on one side of the room, and the dresser next to it was lined with sex toys, ranging from vibrators to whips and a tray lined with coke and pills. She mentally added brothel and drug den to the list of activities available at this establishment, and when she spotted a young girl walking down the hall, she lost her shit.

"Don Carlo is rolling over in his grave right now," she said, the words spilling out before she could filter them.

"It's true, he never approved of making money off what he called 'carnal pleasures,' but he was talking about prostitution. That's not what's happening here."

"Right." She pointed to where she'd seen the girl. "You're telling me you don't provide the 'entertainment'?"

"Oh her. She's decoration. Nothing more." Dominique placed a hand on her hip. "I never took you for being judgy, but you must've picked that up from Siobhan."

Neal winced inwardly at the continued snipes at her boss, but if she was going to get Dominique to continue to confide in her, she knew she needed to play it up. "I'm my own person."

"Then judge for yourself. This place," Dominique waved her arm in a sweeping gesture, "is a pleasure center. We provide the setting and guests make their own fun. We charge memberships and members can bring guests for an extra fee. You would never guess what people will pay for a safe, private space to be uninhibited."

It sounded rational when she said it, but Neal wasn't convinced Dominique had shared everything. How many members would she need just to pay the rent, let alone provide the booze and gambling stakes? She decided to toss a log on the fire. "Siobhan thinks you siphoned off the family fortune. Is that what you used to buy this?"

Dominique's eyes flashed and Neal felt the impact like a slap on the face.

"Don't talk to me about family. And don't believe the lies Siobhan has told you." She pointed at her chest. "*I* am the firstborn child of Don Carlo Mancuso, and I'm the only one authorized to conduct the family business now that he is gone. You think I haven't heard the rumors? Well, I can promise you they are nothing more than that. Siobhan is not his daughter, no matter how much he loved her. She was an orphaned child, worthy of pity, but nothing more. She has already taken more than she deserved in terms of my father's attention and resources, but he's gone now and there's nothing for her here anymore."

Neal considered her next words carefully, not wanting to risk sparking Dominique's anger, but also wanting to put this conversation behind them. She shrugged like it was of little consequence to her who was running things. "Not my family, not my problem."

"It could be. Your family, I mean."

Whoa. Not the response she'd been expecting. She studied Dominique's face looking for a smirk, a wink—some hint of sarcasm, but she saw only a sincere and pleading expression reflected back at her. Was it possible that the death of her father had caused Dominique to grow a heart?

Doubtful, but she had to know more, and she could hear Siobhan's voice whispering in her ear, urging her to play along. She turned in place to take in the room and then faced Dominique again. "I have to admit it looks like you have a good thing going, but one play place isn't going to rebuild your empire. And if you've aligned with Mikhail, then your days are numbered because he's got more enemies than friends."

Dominique laughed. "Please. You think this one club is it? This is one of a dozen already in place with more to come. And you don't need to worry about Petrov. He is a tool to be used and then discarded when the time comes. Trust me. Siobhan may have been sitting at the right-hand of power all these years, but I learned as much or more from my father than she did." She gestured for Neal to join her on the couch. "Now, let's discuss your role and compensation. I know for fact you've never been paid what you're worth." She pointed to Neal's watch. "Tokens are meant to keep you satisfied in the moment. I'm prepared to show you what real value means."

Neal looked down at the Rolex Siobhan had gifted her for Christmas last year. She'd never thought a timepiece would make her feel special, but it had. Maybe it had been a token, but she'd believed it had been a reward for loyalty and an affirmation she was part of the inner circle.

Yet, in all these years, she never promoted you, never brought you into the family.

It wasn't her decision to make until now.

She had influence greater than anyone else in Don Carlo's orbit. The difference is she needs you for more than making sure she doesn't get shot or run over or blown up.

The back and forth continued and she could almost see the cartoonish angel and devil arguing out her destiny while she waited to see who won.

"Are you ready?"

She tore her attention away from her inner conflict, back to Dominique. "Ready?"

Dominique sighed. "To find out how much I value your participation in this new enterprise." She reached into her tiny handbag and pulled out a folded piece of paper and pressed it into Neal's hand. "Take a minute with his. I'll be right back."

Neal stared at the paper in her hand, certain whatever it contained would be life-altering for whoever read the contents. She waited until she was sure Dominique had left the room before slowly unfolding the note.

You're worth more than they ever paid you, but I understand why they never wanted you to feel that way. I spent a lot of time wondering what would be beyond your wildest dreams and then I added a healthy sum to the total. You decide if I got it right.

Neal read the rest three times through to be certain she wasn't seeing things, but each pass was the same. So. Many. Zeros. But it wasn't just the amount that had her attention. She recognized the first line of Dominique's note for the bait it was, but the hook wriggled into her thoughts and tore at the unquestioning loyalty she'd given to Siobhan and Don Carlo.

They saved you. They saved your family.

It was true. They had saved her at a time when her world had come crashing down around her, but was a lifetime of service too much to pay?

You're becoming a made member of the family.

Again true, but what family was left and who was the true heir to the dynasty? Was it Siobhan or Dominique? Apparently, Dominique and her sister, Celia, had already moved to reestablish the Mancuso name in the underworld of Dallas. Yes, they were engaged in pursuits Don Carlo would not have approved of, but he was old school and times had changed. Siobhan had skipped out with an undercover agent who'd sworn to take the family down without giving her the courtesy of telling her where she was going or how to get in touch other than the cryptic note and cash at her apartment. *You're worth more than they ever paid you, but I understand why they never wanted you to feel that way.* Unease curled its way up her spine. Dominique wasn't wrong. Everyone wanted something from her. Siobhan. Royal. Ana. And she wasn't sure who to trust. She needed some distance from all of them to clear her head. She glanced around, but Dominique hadn't reappeared. There were probably cameras all over this place, so she feigned a leisurely pace around the room and then ducked into the main hallway and out the door. She didn't have a car or a plan, but she knew exactly where she needed to go.

CHAPTER THIRTEEN

Ana pressed the button for the penthouse and slid in the keycard, noting the envious looks from the other occupants of the elevator. Would they be jealous if they knew that twice today, she'd used her wiles to obtain keys to rooms that were not her own? This one in particular had exhausted her charm. Thank God she had plenty of practice at feigning interest in insecure men.

Hopefully, her acting had been worth the trouble. She had no idea if Siobhan would be in her apartment. It would certainly be a bold move if she was since the FBI likely had it under surveillance, but she had to start somewhere if she was going to escape from Mikhail and whatever he had planned for their future, and Siobhan was the most likely person to know where Neal might be.

She stepped off the elevator and rang the bell. Royal, Siobhan's lover, answered the door and positioned her body so that Ana couldn't see inside.

"What are you doing here?"

"I could ask the same of you," Ana replied. "Isn't it likely your former employer would be looking for you here?"

She cocked her head. "Or perhaps they are not your former employers at all and you are leading them exactly where you want them to go?"

"Do you really care either way, Anastasia?"

Ana stared at her for a moment, half admiring the risks Royal was taking to be with the one she loved and half believing it was all an act and she'd surprise them all by announcing she'd never left her undercover role. She'd watch her back with this one, but she couldn't let her see any trace of weakness if she wanted to get what she'd come for. "No. I do not. But I would like to speak to the woman in charge." She looked over Royal's shoulder. "Is she in?"

"I am."

Siobhan appeared behind Royal, her expression neutral like it was commonplace to have the wife of her sworn enemy show up at her house. She placed a hand on Royal's bicep and gave her what looked like a gentle squeeze as if to say "I got this."

"Hello, Siobhan."

"What do you want?"

"What I want is not a conversation for hallways," Ana replied, matching her terse tone.

"In case you hadn't noticed, this is a very private hallway. And anything you have to say to me, you can say in front of Royal."

"I find it curious you trust a woman who pledged an oath to bring your family to ruin, yet you do not trust one who comes in peace, offering an alliance that could be most beneficial to you."

Siobhan shrugged. "I've spent years developing a keen sense of who can be trusted and who cannot."

"You need longer to fully develop your skills because you should trust me."

"And why is that?"

"Because I've come here to tell you that something has happened to Neal." She spotted a quick flash of concern dart across Siobhan's face, but she masked it as quickly as it had appeared. This time it was Royal who squeezed her lover's arm, a gesture of comfort and support. Ana couldn't remember the last time someone had touched her in such a way. Wait. It had been Neal. At Sanctuary, the first time they met, after Neal had spilled her drink all over her. She'd been flirting, of course, but the way she acted after had been sweet and tender and Ana hadn't realized it had left a lasting impression.

Or had she? Would she be here if it hadn't?

It was a concern for another day.

"Are you going to tell me more or simply stand in our doorway and daydream?"

Ana clawed her way back from her thoughts and forced her attention back to Siobhan. She caught the use of the word "our" and made a mental note to trend lightly around the subject of Royal since Siobhan was apparently in deep enough to invite Royal to live with her. "I was supposed to meet Neal, but Dominique beat me to it. Now Neal is missing and she's not responding to my calls or texts."

Siobhan looked at Royal who nodded and opened the door wider and made a sweeping gesture with her arm. Ana walked into the penthouse, admiring Siobhan's sleek and subtle taste—the polar opposite of Mikhail's opulent display of all things white and gold, complete with real bearskin rugs and other elaborate and tasteless furnishings. His lack of taste was stifling.

Siobhan pointed to the couch, and she sat down but didn't get comfortable.

"Drink?"

She started to say no, still determined not to relax her guard, but there was a difference between losing control and taking the edge off and she decided to walk that line. "Whisky if you have it."

Siobhan grimaced. "Oh, I have plenty of that. Your husband has made sure of that. He's cut off access to our distributors which leaves us with too much inventory and nothing to do with it. Not a problem your cash can solve."

"Not true," Ana said. "You can buy plenty of loyalty with the money I provided."

"This isn't Russia," Siobhan replied. "The loyalty will last only until the money is spent and then they will be back for more. It's capitalism at its finest."

"Then tell me what I can do to help you."

Siobhan looked over at Royal who took up the baton. "How about you start by telling us what your plans are?"

"I came to tell you about Neal. I thought you would care if something happened to one of your employees."

"Neal is not an employee. She's a member of this family."

Ana nodded. "You mean like one of your captains?"

"It's more than that," Siobhan said. "But yes. She's a capo."

It was a strange word, but she got the gist. Ana brought the subject back around. "Your capo has gone missing." She explained about the arranged meeting at the hotel and what Lauren had seen, noting a flicker of recognition when Ana mentioned Lauren's name. "I've tried to reach her, but my calls go directly to voice mail and she's not responding to my texts."

"Maybe she's just not that into you," Royal said, interjecting herself into the conversation for the first time.

Ana bristled. "Maybe your loyalty isn't what it should be."

"Would you like to tell me what you mean by that?" Royal asked, her voice brewing with anger.

"Do I really need to?" Ana gestured to Siobhan. "You've obviously cast a spell over your girlfriend, but I'm not so easily fooled, and I doubt Neal is either. If you truly left your calling as a federal officer, why aren't they breaking down doors to punish you for it?"

Royal stepped closer, but Siobhan reached for her arm and pulled her back. Surprisingly, she backed off and took a seat.

"Ana, you need to watch your tone in my home," Siobhan said. "As I said before, this isn't Russia and the FBI isn't the KGB. They aren't going to break down doors in the dead of night to whisk citizens away for alleged crimes." She gave her a wry smile. "Besides, Royal has excellent legal counsel and moves are already being made to protect her. I will not tolerate you questioning the loyalty of anyone in my family."

Ana nodded. She didn't want to foreclose any further discussion, but she wasn't entirely convinced. She pivoted to a related issue. "How about Dominique? She's your half-sister, right? Are we not allowed to question her loyalty?"

"Dominique is an entirely different matter. When I speak of family, I'm not talking about blood."

"Yet blood is how you have the claim to run the Mancuso business now, correct?"

"I have earned my right to sit at the head of the table. I don't need Mancuso blood to fuel my sense of duty."

"But it doesn't hurt, right?"

Siobhan smiled again. "No, it does not. Although, when it comes to Dominique, I'm sure the fact that we are related rankles her even more than usual. She's a prime example of blood not having anything to do with loyalty."

"Precisely the reason you should be concerned about her spiriting Neal away."

"Surely, you can understand why I would question your motivation to tell me this. You are the family of my family's enemy."

It was a fair question, but Ana knew exactly how to make Siobhan understand. "Like you, I do not define family by blood or forced formalities. I have chosen to come here, to offer you this information about one of your own." She stood. "If you choose not to act, then that tells me all I need to know about how you treat your family and where your loyalties lie." She pointed to the door. "I'll let myself out."

She'd walked the short distance and had her hand on the door handle when Siobhan called out.

"Wait."

Ana stayed in place for a moment, assessing her choices. She didn't trust either Siobhan or Royal, but for some reason she couldn't name, she trusted Neal and Neal was unflinchingly loyal to Siobhan. If she left now, she could try to find Neal on her own or start over with a different plan, but she'd sipped a taste of freedom and she didn't think she could swallow the idea of starting from scratch with a new plan to break free of Mikhail. The people in this room might not be loyal to her, but they were a means to an end, and judging by their rejection of overtures from Mikhail to join his business, they had some moral compass. With Neal in the wind and no longer in charge, she could either trust Siobhan and Royal or walk away. Was it even a choice?

CHAPTER FOURTEEN

Neal rapped on the door and waited, half hoping no one would answer. It had been years since she'd been here. Guilt told her it was more than she realized, but nothing had changed about the outside appearance of her childhood home. The paint was still peeling, the wooden slats on the porch were still old and rotting. No matter how much money she sent, nothing ever stayed in shape. Cash couldn't buy caring and it never would.

She knocked one more time and, after a moment, started to walk away. It had been a silly impulse that had brought her here, like returning to the scene of a crime ever benefited the criminal. She could only blame all the focus lately on the disintegration of the Mancuso family for causing her to crave familial bonds of her own, but she should've known better than to think her troubled past would suddenly morph into an idyllic memory.

"Neal?"

She instantly recognized the voice but hesitated before turning around in order to school her features into what she hoped was a neutral expression. She turned and forced a smile. "Hi, Mom."

"Oh my goodness. Oh my goodness." Ida Walsh raised her hands to punctuate each exclamation. "Get in here right now." She reached for Neal's arm. "Right now. Oh my goodness."

It was too late to escape now. She stepped toward the door, but her mother grabbed her into her arms before she could cross the threshold. She submitted to the tight hug and forced herself to take long, slow breaths, hoping it hadn't been a mistake to come here.

When her mom finally released her grip, she followed her inside. Unlike the outside, the inside of the house had changed over the years. The furnishings were new and the floors were covered with luxury vinyl tile, although Neal failed to see anything luxurious about it. Still, it was a step up from the worn and tattered carpet that it replaced. The walls were bulging with shelves full of what her mom called "collectibles," better known as junk purchased from the television shopping networks, purchases financed with the money she sent home every month. She sniffed the air. "Something's different."

Her mom reached for a case on the table next to her recliner, and proudly thrust it toward her. "I quit smoking. Found this instead. Comes in all kinds of flavors."

Neal unzipped the case to find a vape and several cartridges. A whiff of fake pineapple scent wafted from the inside and she turned her head away.

"Don't you go using that," her mom said. "It's my favorite. Piña colada. Almost makes me think I'm sitting on the beach, catching rays." She tossed her hair and batted her eyelashes to emphasize the point.

Neal set the case down, praying her mom wouldn't fire up the vape while she was here and resolving that she wouldn't be here for long, no matter what. This house, her family, had always been stifling, but she'd been away so long, she'd allowed herself to forget exactly how suffocating it was to be immersed in a past that was so far removed from what she'd become.

What would Ana think if she could see her now? Ana, who lived in an opulent mansion, dripping with expensive furnishings.

Siobhan had seen this place and she didn't judge.

Siobhan was different. She'd grown up in the Mancuso mansion, but as the child of the cook, not as the rightful heir to the family fortune. Besides, when Siobhan had been here, she'd had one purpose—to collect the debt Neal owed the family. She wouldn't have given a shit where she'd come from as long as she did her duty.

Because all you are to her is a servant.

Dominique's words burrowed past the security she'd allowed herself to feel all these years. Her admonition struck a chord because it was true. She'd grown up dirt poor with a mother who thought all the fine things in life could be ordered from QVC, and a father she'd never know. Her sister had been her only comfort, but fate had whisked her away. Her only talents were her height and her ability to shoot a basketball with incredible accuracy, and those gifts had fallen short of allowing her to escape this place. It wasn't until she threw everything away that she'd found a way out. She'd never questioned the decision to throw the championship game or the pledge to pay Don Carlo back for saving her life, but if she could go back and make different choices from the very beginning, what would her life be like now?

Neal took a long, deep breath. She owed a deep, deep debt to Siobhan and Don Carlo—there was no question that was true. The only question was whether the debt would ever be repaid and what happened after that. Would she be free to leave? To strike out on her own and find a life that didn't rely on protecting someone else's? Sure, Siobhan was making her a capo, but a capo was supposed to have a piece of the action. From what she could tell, the show was nearly over.

"Just you wait until you see what I made for dinner."

Her mother's words jerked her back to the present, and a wave of nausea struck. "I'm sure whatever it is will be great, but I can't stay. I stopped by on my way to see Sarah." She pushed past the grimace her mother reflected her way. "Visiting hours will end soon."

"She won't know you're there." She shrugged. "But if you want to waste your time pretending to have a conversation with her instead of spending it with me, that's fine. It's not like anything you ever did made sense. Dropping out of school and moving away. Leaving us here to fend for ourselves."

She kept up the rant in between long puffs of the pineapple vape, and Neal started moving to the door. She should've known better than to think anything had changed. Fend for herself? Ida hadn't fended for herself in years, and as for Sarah, her room at the home cost more in a year than Ida would make in a lifetime.

The lack of gratitude used to make her mad, but now it only made her sad. Her mom had been so excited when she'd received the scholarship to Tulane. She'd been certain Neal was destined to play professional ball. She'd gone on and on about how they would finally be secure. They could take care of Sarah, buy a bigger house. When she'd won the championship only to have her leg broken, she'd been devastated, but her mom went next-level catastrophe. She even accused her of sabotaging "their" future, as if she had anything to do with Neal's success in the arena.

She opened the door and waited a moment to see if Ida would calm down long enough for her to say good-bye, but she'd disappeared into the kitchen and was still on a tear. "Bye, Mom," Neal yelled into the void and she stepped out onto the porch. When she'd arrived, every detail about its disrepair was nudging her to send money to spruce the place up. Now, all she wanted to do was burn it to the ground along with all her memories of this life. She'd go see Sarah, but this would be the very last time she'd show up at her mother's house.

The drive to the home was so short it felt silly not walking, but she didn't want to leave her car at Ida's. She'd picked the place for its proximity to her mother, thinking she'd be visiting often, but she had a feeling that wasn't the case. Ida had never been maternal, and any kind of illness made that abundantly clear. Her remark about Sarah not recognizing her told Neal that Ida probably didn't make it by very often at all, which was probably for the best.

She parked the car in the visitors' lot and had her choice of spots. When she reached the front door, she glanced around, certain she was being watched. She didn't see anyone nearby, but as soon as she walked inside, she heard a voice call her name. She turned to see Ana standing about six feet away. What the hell?

Ana turned in her direction and their eyes met. Neal was completely captivated, and she had no idea how long she'd been under Ana's spell before her brain interjected a loud *What is she doing here?*

"You're okay."

Neal heard the heavy relief in Ana's words. "Of course."

"I came to the hotel, but you weren't there. I asked you to wait for me."

So that's what this was about? Neal bristled at the scolding. "You sent a prostitute with a note. That's not the same thing as showing up yourself. I decided not to wait around."

"You left with Dominique Mancuso. Lauren was under the impression you did so under duress." Ana frowned. "Forgive me for thinking you were in trouble."

Guilt edged into Neal's anger, but she shoved it aside. She didn't have to explain herself to Ana no matter how much money she'd infused into the family business. Besides, it wasn't like it was her family. Sure, Siobhan had said she was made now, but did she even have the authority to make it so? All she had was her word.

Which had always been enough before you met with Dominique.

Everything about her meeting with Dominique had left her agitated and she hadn't even begun to process Dominique's offer. She wished she could talk to someone about it, but there wasn't anyone she could trust, which led her back to what the hell was Ana doing here? "How did you know I would be here?"

"I didn't, but Siobhan gave me a list of places she thought you might be if you weren't with Dominique. I took a guess this would be the most likely one."

Neal took a moment to process the fact that Ana had been concerned enough about her disappearance to go directly to Siobhan, and that Siobhan had shared this aspect of her private life with a virtual stranger. "And she decided you were wrong about Dominique taking me hostage?"

Ana shrugged. "She decided if that were the case, she had the appropriate resources to handle it. I'm quite certain she sent me off looking in other directions because she doesn't want me to have any contact with her half-sister."

It sounded weird to have Siobhan referred to as Dominique's half-sister, but also accurate. "Maybe she's decided Dominique isn't a force of evil after all."

Ana narrowed her eyes. "Or perhaps that's what you've decided. Since it appears you're not Dominique's hostage after all, have you formed an alliance with her? Are you here doing her bidding? Trust me when I tell you that she and Mikhail are up to no good. Whatever they've told you is designed to get you to help them, and them alone."

"And you came all this way to tell me that?"

"That surprises you? Did you not read my note?"

Shit. Neal reached into her pocket and drew out the folded card. She'd completely forgotten about it in her haste to get out of town, and she felt strange reading it while Ana was standing right there. "Why don't you tell me what it says?"

Ana reached out her hand and placed it over Neal's, drawing it back down to her pocket. "Not now. Read it later when you are ready. For now, tell me why we are here at this place." She gestured to the door of the facility.

Neal hesitated. The only person outside of her family who knew about her sister was Siobhan. Sarah was a vulnerability she'd prefer no one ever be able to use against her again, but she heard genuine concern in Ana's voice at finding her here, at wondering why she was at this place. She'd spent the entire drive here wishing she had someone to confide in, and the words simply spilled out. "My sister has lived here for many years. She's completely disabled and she probably doesn't even know where she is or who I am, but I need to see her."

"Of course you do." Ana looked around appearing completely nonplussed. "Do you want me to leave you alone or would you like some company on your visit?"

The second option wasn't anything she would have thought possible, but the idea of not having to face Sarah's situation by herself was a huge relief. She reached out a hand. "Come on."

They signed in at the front desk and a few minutes later, Danielle, an orderly Neal had met on several occasions, led them back to a room at the far end of the building. This facility was the best one in the region, but Neal hated the institutional feel, the smell, the sterilized everything about the place. Sarah's life had had such promise before the accident, but now it was reduced to a bed and a feeding tube. She should visit more, but it was a painful reminder of both their wasted lives. What would Sarah think if she knew what she did for a living now? Sarah who'd sat in the front row at her games, cheering louder than anyone else in the crowd.

She stopped at the door to Sarah's room and turned to Ana. "You don't have to come in."

"Do you want me with you?"

"I don't want to be alone."

"Then I'm here for you. Why can't you trust that I know what I want?"

It was a good question, and the answer was likely that she didn't know what she wanted for herself so she was projecting, but that sounded a little too much like psychobabble for her to admit out loud. Neal grabbed the door handle. "Come on then."

Sarah was propped up in bed, her eyes vacant and unmoving. She wore a royal blue blouse that Neal recognized as one she'd bought for her birthday last year and she figured Danielle, who she generously tipped whenever she visited, probably dressed her in it when she learned Neal was here for a visit. Sarah had always loved the color and Neal liked to think she knew she was wearing it now, but the truth was that while it made her feel better, the blouse probably had no effect on Sarah whatsoever.

She strode over to the bed and took her sister's hand. She owed it to her to continue to pretend. "Hey, Sarah, it's been a while, right?" She pointed over her shoulder. "I have company today. This is Ana."

Ana waved. "Hello, Sarah, it's nice to meet you."

Neal nodded and Ana stepped closer. "I like to think she can hear us," she whispered.

"I'm sure she can," Ana replied. "The brain is very resilient, even when the body is not."

Neal flashed back on her mother's words denying that fact, and appreciated even more that Ana was here with her. She pointed at the chairs Danielle had set up next to the bed. "Let's sit. Sarah gets antsy when we're standing."

"Of course."

Neal watched Ana settle in the seat. She appreciated the way Ana was so matter-of-fact about this visit and Sarah's condition. What would she think if she knew why Sarah was confined to this place, unable to care for herself or live out the life she'd dreamed? Not for the first time, Neal considered it karmic that she'd sacrificed her own dreams trying to make up for the fact Sarah had lost hers. They'd both wound up with nothing, and paying for Sarah's care and these few and far between visits were slim tokens of retribution.

"What do you two usually talk about?"

Ana looked at her intently as she asked the question, like she truly wanted to know the answer. "We have a series of favorite topics. Current events, except for politics. Best new restaurants, but I kind of suck at it because food is really not my thing." She paused. "Sometimes, I read to her. The last book was *Gone Girl*."

"Ah, you are a mystery buff."

"I wouldn't say I'm a buff, but I do enjoy suspense." Neal looked at Sarah. "She's always loved them, and I like to think she reacts when I read."

"I'm sure you're right. Why don't you read to her now?"

Neal held out her hands. "I don't have a book with me. This trip was kind of last minute."

Ana rolled her eyes. "We'll talk about the reason behind your desire to escape Dallas in a hurry more later, but let's find a book for you to read to your sister." She pulled out her phone, punched a few buttons, and handed it over.

Neal took it from her and stared at the book app on the screen, already loaded with the latest from J.M. Redmann. Surprised that Ana was familiar with the lesbian detective series, she looked up at her and spotted a trace of a smile. "You already had this loaded on your phone?"

"Yes, and welcome to this century where you don't have to lug around a hard copy of a book you want to read. How old are you anyway?"

Neal smiled at the ironic reference to the difference in their ages. She was twenty-eight, but most days the weight of her responsibilities left her feeling a decade older. She knew from her research that Ana was in her forties though the exact age was hard to pin down. "I like the feel of a book in my hand."

"Me too, but if others were to find the books I like to read lying around the house, it would cause problems."

Neal held up the phone. "Like this one?"

"Exactly like that one." Ana shrugged. "Anyway, I thought that because we're near New Orleans, it would be the perfect choice."

Neal had more questions. Many more, but she was here for Sarah and now was not the time, so she echoed Ana's words from earlier. "We'll talk more about your penchant for lesbian detectives, but now I'm going to read to my sister. Would you like to stay?"

Ana's smile was broad this time. "I was hoping you would ask."

CHAPTER FIFTEEN

Ana watched Neal read to her sister, impressed by her animation and expressiveness. Sarah might have no idea they were in the room, but Ana felt every word come alive. She'd read the book a dozen times, in secret, holed up in her suite at the house where no one else could see or judge, but hearing someone else read it aloud was like an affirmation, an awakening. She wasn't alone. Others read and enjoyed these stories, and they reflected a life that was real or could be if she could find her way out of the one she was in. And she had to.

"I think that's enough for today."

Ana looked up at Neal who held the phone out toward her. Sarah's head had rolled to the side and her eyes were droopy, and Ana glanced at the page count on her phone. She must've wandered off into thought while Neal had read judging by how far into the book she'd gotten. "You left off at a really good part."

Neal smiled. "I know, but I think it's more about the act of being read to for her than the story itself."

She stood, leaned over, and kissed her sister on the cheek. Ana watched the tender, personal moment, feeling like she should glance away, but unable to resist witnessing this side of Neal. When Neal looked her way, her eyes were wet with tears and Ana started to go to her, to comfort her, but as she drew closer, Neal held up a hand and pointed to the door.

"We should go."

Ana followed her to the door and watched while Neal tracked down the orderly who'd ushered them in. She stood a few feet away while they had a whispered conversation that ended with Neal pressing a wad of cash into the orderly's hand. She had many questions. Now wasn't the time to ask them, but she resolved to learn more about this enigmatic woman who seemed to have given her life over to protecting everyone's interests at the expense of her own.

They walked out of the facility, side by side. Ana paused when they reached the parking lot. She'd taken a car service from the airport and sent them away, unsure what the day would hold and impulsively anxious to get to Neal. Poor planning on her part.

Neal looked back over her shoulder. "What's wrong?"

Ana grimaced. "I didn't plan past finding you, and it appears I'm stranded. She held up her phone. I'm going to see if I can call for a ride."

"You know they have apps for that."

"Don't look at me like I'm a hundred years old. I know they do. I also know they keep records and anyone who might be able to access my phone will be able to track my movements."

Neal nodded. "Good point." She held up her keys. "Good thing I have a car." She turned and started walking in the other direction. She was a few steps away when she called out, "Are you coming?"

Ana walked briskly to make up the distance, both relieved to have a ride and exhilarated at the idea of spending more time with Neal.

"I'm starving," Neal said. "Are you hungry?"

"I am. Dinner's on me. As payment for the ride."

"Maybe you should wait to see how the ride goes before you make promises about paying. Louisiana is full of swamps. I could be taking you to the middle of nowhere and leaving you there."

"I doubt that."

Neal cocked her head. "Is that so. Why?"

"Because a woman who cares for her sister the way you do wouldn't have the heart to abandon a stranger who was in need."

"You just spent an hour listening to me read to my disabled sister. I hardly think you're a stranger."

"All the more reason you won't abandon me." Ana held out her hand. "Take me somewhere decadent and expensive where we can talk in private." She waited through the uncomfortable silence until Neal finally reached out and grabbed her hand, clenching tightly as she led her to the car. Mikhail often steered her around, in a display of ownership, but this was different. It was like Neal was holding to a lifeline and Ana squeezed back to let her know she'd found one. Neal was supposed to be saving her, but after what she'd just witnessed, it might be Neal who needed to be rescued.

They drove for a while, past several shabby, tired towns, through a bustling downtown that spilled out into a neighborhood full of large, stately homes with bright green manicured landscapes. Ana took in the gorgeous gardens and the old-fashioned trolley and was transported. *This place is magical. I could stay here. Never go back.*

As quickly as the thought appeared, a dozen objections emerged to rob it of life. It's too close. He would find me here.

I can't leave until everything is in place, and Mikhail being left alive in order to hunt her down wasn't an option.

They pulled up in front of a building with a subtle sign, *Blanchard's*. She'd read a feature piece on the restaurant in the airline magazine, and was pleased with Neal's choice though she feared that without a reservation they were unlikely to get in.

She needn't have worried. After they left the car with the valet and stepped into the crowded lobby, Neal told the hostess she needed a party of two for a friend of Muriel Casey. The hostess's hesitation was barely noticeable, but Ana had developed a keen ability to read micro expressions, a skill that came in handy when dealing with Mikhail and his crew. The woman picked up a phone, whispered a few words, and faced them with a broad smile. "It would be my pleasure to seat you at one of our finest tables."

Ana waited until they were seated, and the hostess was out of sight before leaning close to Neal. "Do you know the Caseys?"

"I do." Neal pointed at the menu. "You should know that I'm starving, and I plan to order the most expensive meal on the menu."

Most people who knew the head of a celebrated organized crime family well enough to invoke the family name in order to get a table for dinner would be happy to share that fact, but Neal seemed completely disinterested in discussing the issue. "Cain Casey has quite the reputation."

"She's earned it. Trust me."

The waiter appeared and Neal ordered a Jameson's, neat, a plate of oysters, and a large steak. When she finished her order, Ana handed the waiter the menu and simply said, "Same."

Neal raised an eyebrow. "You don't strike me as a steak girl."

"I'm not a girl at all, so that makes sense."

"You know what I meant."

Now it was Ana's turn to raise her eyebrows. "I don't. Care to fill me in?"

Neal's face reddened and she took a sip of water. When she finally set the glass down, she said, "I guess you seem like more of a vodka soda and salad kind of *woman*." She waved her hand from Ana's head to her feet to further emphasize the point.

Ana laughed. "You're not wrong about the vodka, but I would never weaken it with cheap carbonated water. And you think we survive Russian winters on salad?" She shook her head. "You Americans have so much to learn."

"How did you wind up here anyway? Isn't your family a big deal in Russia?"

The question caught her off guard since she'd expected they would talk about Sarah and Neal's encounter with Dominique and her plan to break from Mikhail. The origin of how she'd come to be in the States in the first place was a sore spot she didn't much care to revisit. But Neal had shared a vulnerable moment with her today and it would only be fair for her to do the same.

The waiter returned then with their drinks and slipped away quickly as if he sensed they were on the cusp of a private conversation. Ana took a deep swallow and let the alcohol's warm blaze burn through her reticence. "My family is rich and powerful. A big deal, as you say, but there are always limits to what can be achieved in Russia because the government doesn't allow anyone to get too successful for fear they will seek freedoms that allow them to become even more powerful in a way that can no longer be controlled."

Neal nodded. "Communism at its finest."

"Communism isn't the worst idea, but it doesn't work when individual ambition is rewarded. People begin to believe they do not need to rely on anyone else for their success and therefore should not have to share the spoils of their work. It all falls apart and the rich become richer and the poor despair."

"You still haven't answered the question."

"I'm getting there." Ana took another sip of her drink. "My family became a little too successful and the Kremlin stepped in to take more than their fair share. Mikhail's family had already established enterprises abroad, out of Putin's greedy clutches, and an alliance was formed."

"Ah, I see. You married Mikhail for business."

"Yes." She scoured Neal's face, noting the hint of disdain. "You judge me for it."

"I don't."

Ana didn't believe her, but she didn't blame her either. "Our arrangement is about business alone. Nothing more."

"Does your family know you're gay?"

Ana choked mid-swallow and glanced around, but no one at any of the nearby tables seemed to have heard or registered Neal's question. She'd asked it like it was a topic they'd discussed before and one of minimal consequence, and her casualness made Ana angry. "Keep your voice down."

"Why?" Neal asked in an over exaggerated whisper. "Is it a secret?"

"You wouldn't understand."

"Try me."

"In my country, you can be locked up, spirited away for such things. Marrying Mikhail was more than simply duty to my family. I did it to hide who I am."

"But now you want to break free."

"It was inevitable. Coming to this country allowed me to see that there are possibilities I could not have envisioned for myself back in Mother Russia. At some point, Mikhail will be called back by his family and his younger brother will take over here. If I do not make my move before then, then I will return with him, and I don't know that I will ever be free."

"Well, that explains why you're so desperate to work with your husband's mortal enemy."

"I have been planning for a long time, but circumstance is the reason I look to you and Siobhan now. With Don Carlo's death and the divide in the family, it's the perfect opportunity to form new alliances."

Neal winced at the words and Ana instantly regretted how callous they sounded. "My apologies. I know you both lost someone close to you. I didn't mean to make it sound like a boon."

"It's not just Siobhan and I who lost someone close. Dominique and Celia Mancuso have lost a father as well."

Warning bells went off at the mention of Dominique and Neal's ostensible deference to their feelings. She had to tread carefully here. "So, it's true. Your visit with Dominique was a friendly one."

A flicker of surprise crossed Neal's face. "I'm not sure I would call it friendly, but it was interesting. I figured you'd know more about it since she's in business with your husband."

"Can we agree to stop calling him that?"

"I get it. You want to stop thinking of him like a person so when you make the call to end his life, you don't feel so bad about it." Neal shrugged. "I'm not sure I can give you what you want."

Ana looked around at the other tables, relieved again no one appeared to be interested in their conversation since Neal insisted on being so direct. It was time for her to be direct too. "You think I'm asking you to help me for selfish reasons. Because I'm trapped in a marriage that was arranged for me, because as long as I remain trapped, I cannot be myself, cannot love who I want." She paused. "All of that is true, but it's not the whole story." She took a drink to gather herself.

"Mikhail is not a person. He's a monster. He makes his money by trafficking young girls into prostitution and selling drugs on a massive scale. Did Dominique show you the hidden buildings with the fancy rooms where she will help him carry out his atrocities? Where dressed-up wealthy people will go to indulge their fantasies, not caring about the cost of their gratification on those they deem beneath them. Did they offer you an insane amount of money to work with them?"

Neal didn't meet her eyes, which confirmed there was truth in her accusations, but not whether Dominique had been successful in her quest to win Neal over. No longer caring about discretion, Ana reached out and placed her hand on Neal's. "Tell me."

Neal looked up slowly, her eyes reflecting pain and conflict. Ana squeezed her hand gently, determined not to make any sudden movements lest she chase away the version of Neal who seemed to want to be close to her.

"She did offer me a job. A generous offer." Neal paused. "She said a lot of things that were designed to get me to distrust Siobhan and Royal."

Ana was warmed by the level of trust it took for Neal to admit any of those things to her. She pressed forward carefully. "Did it work?"

Neal picked at one of the rolls the waiter had left for them. "I already distrust Royal."

She'd distrusted Royal too, up until the moment Royal and Siobhan had shared with her a list of places they thought Neal might be if she wasn't with Dominique. The list had been short, consisting of only Sanctuary and the small town of Ponchatoula, where Neal had grown up. Ana would've preferred confronting Dominique herself, but Siobhan had pointed out the pitfalls in such an approach, urging her to see that a direct assault on the business partner of the husband she was trying to manipulate would only jeopardize her long-term plans. She had to believe a true enemy wouldn't try to sway her from making such a mistake.

But Neal surely had her own motivations for not trusting Royal, and Ana chose her words carefully. "You're not alone. Is it because she was an FBI agent or is it something else?"

"It started with that, but now I don't know. Everything has changed, and I guess I don't know who to trust anymore."

"You guarded Siobhan for years and you feel like she doesn't need you anymore."

Neal shifted in her seat. "I'm not a child. I don't need to be needed."

Ana started to point out that after what she'd witnessed at the facility this afternoon, being needed seemed to be the hallmark of Neal's life but decided the truth of the statement would fall flat in this moment when Neal was unsure who to trust. Instead, she steered the conversation in a different direction. "Tell me about Sarah. Is she older or younger?"

A shadow crossed Neal's face. "Older. Three years. She was the brains in the family. Accepted to Tulane on an academic scholarship instead of an athletic one."

Ana heard the disdain in Neal's voice. "I've seen clips of you playing basketball. You deserved your scholarship."

"I thought I did. I thought I was on track to go all the way to the WNBA. This," she motioned to indicate her height, "would finally be something to respect rather than something people pointed and laughed at."

She gave a half smile, but her remark was laced with sadness, and Ana wasn't fooled. The story Neal was about to tell was intimate and private and painful. She'd seen the reports on the internet about the star basketball player who lost her scholarship due to severe injuries that occurred off the court, but they were all long on speculation and short on detail, leaving her with more questions than answers. She was no stranger to festering secrets and the sway they held over every aspect of a person's life. It wasn't her business to push Neal, but she told herself it was for Neal's sake as much as her own.

The waiter approached, flanked by an assistant, both of them carrying platters of food. Ana held up a hand before they reached the table and they stopped several feet away. She leaned toward Neal. "Are you hungry?"

Neal sighed. "I should be, but I'm not anymore."

Ana signaled to the waiter. "We need all of this to-go, please. And the check. Thank you." She reached a hand out to Neal. "Come on. I have an idea."

CHAPTER SIXTEEN

Neal recognized the outside of the Hotel Monteleone as Ana pulled the car to a stop at the valet stand. "What are we doing here?"

Ana pointed at the bag of food in the back seat. "Grab that and I'll meet you inside."

Neal complied, too discombobulated by the day's events to process anything other than the simple task. The bellman tried to take the bag from her, but she held on tightly, an act of irrational focus. She climbed the steps and entered the lobby of the grand hotel, spotting Ana at the front desk engaged in a conversation with one of the clerks.

She'd been here before. Once. The night the manager for the Dallas Wings came to speak to her about her plans for after college. Barely into her sophomore year, the conversation had seemed premature, but she had no way of knowing at the time how unnecessary it would become and how much her life would change before she finished out the season.

"Neal."

She looked up to see Ana standing beside her with her hand outstretched. She shifted the bag of food to her other arm, slipped her hand into Ana's, and followed her to the elevator as if it were perfectly natural. Less than twelve hours ago, she'd been at a similar hotel, at Ana's bidding and it felt oddly comforting to bookend the day with a similar event.

A few minutes later, they walked through the door to a spacious suite with a view of the Mississippi River. Ana took the bag of food from Neal and set it on the bar. She removed two glasses from the cabinet and poured from a full bottle of Jameson's that was sitting on the shelf. She handed Neal a glass and pointed across the room. "Let's sit."

Neal followed her to the couch and didn't object when Ana removed her shoes and sat close to her, finding her proximity as soothing as the whisky. More so even.

"You were destined for the WNBA," Ana prompted her.

"I was."

"But something happened."

"So many things."

"Tell me one."

"I was driving when the accident happened." Neal was acutely aware she was starting in the middle of the story, but if she tried to stumble through the beginning, she feared she'd never make it to the end. "I barely even remember it. I heard a loud crash. Screaming. It was Sarah, it was me. It was the other driver. Then sirens and lights and people everywhere, shouting. Loud, grinding noises, sparks. They shoved me into the back of an ambulance and drove away."

"Was Sarah with you?"

Neal slowly shook her head, heavy with hazy memories. "She was still in the car. They worked for an hour to get her loose. The other driver struck us on her side. A direct hit on her door. They told me later he'd run the light. He was running late for a game at the SKC." She laughed. "You'll get the irony in a bit."

Ana reached for her hand. "Tell me about Sarah's injuries."

"She suffered a massive head injury, broken ribs and hip. Her body healed, but the brain did not. There's a one percent chance that one day she'll come to and be able to speak again, but with every day that passes, the possibility goes down. She will probably never recover, but that's a realization that's taken me years to embrace. Right after the accident, I would do anything to make sure she had that chance."

She could tell by the way Ana perked up at the emphasis on the word "anything" that she knew they were at a critical part of the story. She could either stop now or power through. A squeeze to her hand spurred her on.

"The home is expensive. It costs more to give a bed to someone and watch them wither away than it does to house and feed a living family. But I didn't care what it cost because I blamed myself for that night. The other driver blew the light, but it was my call to be driving that route in the first place. I'd forgotten my favorite jacket back at the dorm and I was determined not to go out that night without it. My selfish decision robbed her of the rest of her life."

"You couldn't have known what would happen."

Ana was right, of course, but no matter how many times she'd heard the words, they didn't dull the pain.

"How did you pay for her care?"

"At first there were fundraisers. Everyone came out to help the sister of a basketball player on the rise, but everyone only has so much money to give or attention to pay, and after a while the charity dried up." Neal took a deep drink, waiting for the burn of fortification before her next words.

"I received an offer. From a capo in the Fellini family."

Ana's eyes closed for a moment, and Neal wondered what she must think of her since she'd judged her harshly for the company she'd kept. "I didn't think I had a choice."

"You probably didn't." Ana sighed. "I know how you felt."

"They were generous. Told me it was because they were fans. They wanted to help out."

"But that wasn't all, was it?"

"No, they sent someone later to tell me that the Don needed me to pay up. That I needed to throw the championship game to repay the debt."

"What did they threaten you with?"

"They threatened to dry up the money, but then they added to it that they had photos of me meeting with them and accepting money. They threatened to let slip that I had accepted bribes all along for inside information about the team and our opponents. I was damned if I did and damned if I didn't. The only way I could keep Sarah alive was to do what they wanted."

Ana's brow furrowed. "But you didn't."

Neal smiled. "Someone did their homework. No, I didn't. I was going to, but I couldn't. Sarah would've hated it, no matter what the reason, and I knew I'd always be in their debt."

"They hurt you for breaking the rules."

Neal winced at the memory. "They broke one leg and I'm pretty sure they were planning to break the other when Don Carlo and Siobhan showed up. They'd been at the game and were looking for me, to congratulate me on the win." She could still see the entire scene—a high-def movie always ready to replay. Enzo holding the bat over his head, ready to bring it crashing down while she writhed in pain on the floor beneath him.

"*Stop, or I'll shoot.*"

The words of a cop, but the woman wielding the gun didn't look like any cop Neal had ever seen. She was young and gorgeous and dressed like a model, yet she held the gun with the confidence of a seasoned vet. Enzo didn't drop the bat, but he stepped on her instep with his boot to hold her in place and turned toward the woman.

"*Who the fuck are you?*"

A slow, feral smile slid across the woman's face, and she stepped to the side to reveal a man standing behind her. He was older than she was—her father, perhaps? He held a copy of the program for the game in one hand and a fedora in the other, and he watched the woman with the gun with admiration in his eyes.

"*Who I am isn't important,*" *the woman said. She jerked her chin over her shoulder, keeping the gun trained on Enzo.* "*But that man is Don Carlo Mancuso, and you've offended him greatly by your actions tonight.*"

Enzo scoffed. "*I don't know who either of you think you are, but you're not from around here.*"

"*No, but I am.*"

Neal spotted another woman stepping out of the darkness and another standing behind her. The first one she recognized, preceded by her reputation. She pointed at the bat in Enzo's hand.

"*You should know better than to bring a bat to a gunfight.*" *Cain Casey turned back to the woman behind her.* "*Right, Muriel?*"

"Right, Cain."

Fear flashed in Enzo's eyes at the exchange. "Who are you?"

"I'm certain you already know," Cain said, "Based on the way you flinched when you heard my name." She stepped closer to him. "Are you going to put that bat down or die with it in your hands?"

Slowly, Enzo lowered the bat and set it on the ground. "I don't have a beef with you."

"As of right now, you don't have a beef with anyone," Cain said as she walked over and picked up the bat and handed it to Muriel. "And you're going to leave now, unharmed, for one reason and one reason alone. Can you guess what it is?"

He stared at her and the sweat pouring off his forehead signaled he was in obvious distress. Finally, he shook his head vigorously.

"Because Neal here is under my protection. And she always will be. Do you understand what that means?"

His only answer was a slow nod.

"Excellent. Now go tell your friends." He stayed in place, and she made a shooing motion with her hands. "Go, now."

He abandoned any dignity he might have left and ran off. Neal felt the adrenaline subside and pain ripped through her entire right side. She barely remembered what happened next, but Siobhan had filled her in later. Cain had arranged for transportation to a private clinic where no one would report the nature of her injury to law enforcement and the record of her treatment would be sealed. Siobhan and Don Carlo had moved her to Dallas and given her a job as Siobhan's bodyguard and arranged payment for Sarah's treatment on an ongoing basis. Stunned by the turn her life had taken, she had

*let it all happen, both grateful for their kindness and relief at
not having to make any decisions about her future.*

"So, now you're in their debt?"

"Believe me, I get the irony. Yes, I traded paying back
Enzo for becoming a foot soldier to a different crime family
for life."

"Regrets?"

"I regret taking that drive with Sarah. If we hadn't been
on the road that night, she might be fine and I might be a star
forward in the WNBA." Neal sighed. "I realize how that makes
me sound."

Ana reached for her hand and pulled her into her arms.
"It makes you sound human. Like a person with dreams and
aspirations of her own. Believe me, I know what it's like to
have others decide your fate."

Neal relaxed into Ana's arms, unable to remember the last
time someone had held her for the sole purpose of offering
comfort, but as Ana's fingers played lightly in her hair, her
body heat rose and comfort took a back seat to the growing
arousal spreading through her. She turned and found Ana
looking down at her, her eyes dark with desire. She placed a
hand on Ana's cheek and drew her closer until their lips met,
softly at first and then with the hard press of passion.

The kiss was fiery and fierce, and Neal surrendered to its
intensity, no longer caring about controlling her own destiny if
fate chose to place her in Ana's arms, feeling every delicious
caress of her perfect tongue. She needed release, but more than
that, she needed to feel wanted, not for what she could do, but
for who she was. Still, as Ana began to slowly undress her, she
placed her hand on Ana's and held tight.

"You want me to stop?"

"Far from it. It's just…" She struggled to articulate the conflict. She wanted this. She wanted Ana. Why was she hesitating?

"You don't always have to be the one to fulfill the needs of others," Ana whispered close to her ear. "You deserve more. Let me take care of you."

Was it really that easy? Could she simply submit to this woman who she barely knew? Before her brain could formulate a response, she loosened her grip on Ana's hand and let her hand fall to her side. Ana's gaze followed the move and she smiled in response. She laced their fingers together and tugged Neal upright, leading her across the room. Neal followed, sitting on the edge of the bed as directed, and kept her hands to herself, while Ana finished unbuttoning her shirt.

"You're so beautiful," Ana said as she raked her fingers over Neal's bare abdomen, gently pushing her back so she was lying prone on the bed.

Neal's breath hitched as Ana's hands roamed all over her body. "Beautiful, huh? You really think so?"

A frown flashed across Ana's face and her eyes filled with compassion. "Has someone told you otherwise?"

Neal met her eyes and basked in the kindness she saw reflected back at her. For a second, she'd thought Ana was ready to go beat someone up on her behalf. "No, it's just…" Words were hard. Especially when Ana's fingers dipped into the waist of her pants, lighting every one of her senses on fire. "Not a word I hear a lot." She groaned as Ana unfastened her fly and slid her entire hand between her skin and her now soaked boxer briefs.

"What a travesty," Ana breathed the words against her ear and punctuated her remark with a long, slow stroke of her tongue along the side of her neck while her fingers explored down below. "Because you are undeniably gorgeous."

If she'd even considered denying Ana's declaration, she couldn't because she'd lost the ability to form words the moment Ana dipped a finger into her hot, wet center. For a moment, she hung in the balance between fulfilling her desires and being distracted by the voice inside that whispered words of doubt. *You don't deserve pleasure. Pleasure will make you forget the debt you owe.*

"You feel amazing."

She looked up into Ana's eyes and melted at the affection she witnessed there. They held the virtual embrace for a moment before Ana bent her head and began kissing her breasts in long, slow strokes. The intensity of each caress took her close to the edge and back again, reflecting the pendulum of her feelings. She wanted this. She wanted Ana. But she'd spent a lifetime denying herself out of guilt, out of obligation. Habit told her she should do so again now, but the force of her desire for Ana was too strong to deny, and she arched into Ana's touch, embracing vulnerability for the first time in years and trusting Ana with her soul.

Ana quietly shut the door behind the room service attendant and wheeled the cart further into the room, careful not to wake Neal who'd been sleeping soundly for the past hour. She was in the middle of pouring a cup of coffee when

Neal's sleepy voice startled her into spilling some on the white cloth covering the cart.

"Come back to bed."

Ana smiled. "I will as soon as I pour this coffee. Want some?"

"Yes, please," Neal said. She propped herself up on pillows. "And French toast, and pancakes, and eggs, and bacon. I'm starving and I think you know why."

"Because you didn't eat all of your dinner?" Ana said, pretending to ignore the sly grin on Neal's face.

Neal responded by tossing a pillow in her direction. "Hey, you're going to ruin the beautiful breakfast I ordered you." Ana wheeled the cart closer to the bed. "I wasn't sure if you were a coffee or tea person, so I ordered both."

"Coffee, please." Neal reached over and began lifting the lids on the covered plates. "It looks like you ordered most of the menu." She lifted a piece of bacon and made a show of swooning as she ate.

"As I said, I wasn't sure what you liked."

"I think you might have to stop saying that after last night."

Ana stopped pouring and set the pitcher down. She strode the last few steps to the bed and leaned down, taking Neal's lips in her own, and melted into her touch. Again.

"I'm not big on gambling, but I bet you taste better than anything on that tray," Neal said, gasping when they finally broke for air.

"I don't know about that. All the reviews say the eggs Benedict here are truly indulgent." Ana eased out of Neal's grasp and sorted out the plates, making sure there was a decent split of sweet and savory on each. Not her usual fare of egg whites, low-fat yogurt, and toast, but nothing about this day or last night was usual, and the restrictions she placed on herself seemed silly after spending the night in Neal's arms.

"I'm sure they're great, but if you want the best food in New Orleans, you need to hit the street, not order room service." She took a sip of her coffee. "Have you been here before?"

"First time. Mikhail is the traveler in the family. I'm supposed to stay at home and look pretty. But I've read about it and I've always wanted to come here. Here and New York City. I've flown into the airport there, but I've never gotten to experience the city itself." She closed her eyes for a moment. "I fantasize about high tea at the Baccarat Hotel, and I've only read about it in magazines." She threaded her fingers through Neal's and looked down at their joined hands to hide the look of shame in her eyes. But a moment later, Neal placed a single finger under her chin and coaxed her into looking up.

"What's the matter?"

She wasn't sure really. She was a grown woman, smart and ambitious, but she hadn't been out in the world, hadn't experienced life. What she knew of destinations other than her favorite shopping and dining haunts in Dallas, all came from the pages of a magazine or podcasts listened to while walking on a treadmill—the perfect symbol for a life that went nowhere. She clenched Neal's hand before answering. "Nothing's wrong." In response to Neal's frown, she added, "I promise." She ran her hand down Neal's naked back. "This is perfect."

"Good." Neal patted the covers. "Let's take advantage of this bed until they toss us out."

"Eat first," Ana purred. "You're going to need your strength. And I arranged for a late check out."

Neal stretched her arms over her head. "Perfect."

It was perfect. Ana wanted to suggest they stay in New Orleans for the day, act like tourists, eating and drinking their way through the French Quarter, doing all the touristy things she'd read about in the magazine on the plane, but short-term fun could have long-term consequences for both their futures. If Neal didn't show back up in Dallas, Siobhan and Royal could start to rethink the loyalty they'd placed in her and that could affect the deal she'd made with the Mancusos. And she needed that deal to work now more than ever. Otherwise, Mikhail would always control her destiny, no matter how smart and ambitious she might be. But as she looked into Neal's eyes, she allowed herself the luxury of imagining a future where she controlled her own destiny and was able to live and love for the very first time.

CHAPTER SEVENTEEN

Neal grabbed Ana's hand and held it tight as the elevator doors opened. She'd spoken to Siobhan briefly since she'd returned from New Orleans, but this would be the first time they would be face to face following her trip and she wasn't sure what to expect.

Ana hung back as they reached the door.

"What is it?" Neal asked.

"I wasn't invited."

"You don't have to be. You're with me."

"No offense, but I'm not entirely sure that will be a good thing. They may have agreed to accept my help, but deep down, they think I'm trying to use you."

Neal leaned down and grazed Ana's cheek with her lips. "You were definitely using me last night," she whispered. "And I loved it." No matter what Siobhan and Royal had to say, she was convinced Ana's feelings toward her went beyond physical attraction, and she'd fight anyone who tried to tell her something different. Besides, as much as she hated to admit it, her conversation with Dominique had left her feeling unsettled when it came to Siobhan. Having Ana by her side signaled she had options and was not to be taken for granted. She tugged on Ana's hand. "Come on."

Royal answered the door, holding it open only a few inches and guarding the open space. Neal spent a second resenting how she'd supplanted her role before the rational part of her brain kicked in. She wasn't a bodyguard anymore, and the only person she needed to protect was herself, and with that realization came a sense of relief.

"Are you going to let us in?" Neal asked, not bothering to hide the challenge in her voice.

Royal gave Ana a once-over but didn't say anything as she eased the door open and motioned them to come inside. Siobhan was on the couch with her laptop, furiously clicking away on the keyboard. Neal hung back for a moment, not sure if her new role meant she should take a seat or stand to the side.

Siobhan looked up. "I'm sorry. I was checking something. Please sit." She smiled at Ana. "I see you were able to find her."

"She did find me." Neal reached for Ana's hand. "Are you ready to accept that we can work together?"

Siobhan shot a very pointed look at their joined hands and met Neal's gaze with an unwavering stare of her own. "The range of things I've come to accept has expanded greatly over the past few months. Do you not trust me to know what is best for this family?"

Neal recognized the tone. She'd heard Siobhan use it in court many times when faced with an adversary who didn't see things her way. But she wasn't an adversary. She was a dedicated and loyal member of this family. "You said you were making me a capo. If that's true, shouldn't you trust me as well?"

Royal stepped forward, like she thought it was her place to intervene and Neal moved to the edge of her seat, ready to take her on. Siobhan held up a hand. "Peace. We want the same things. I'm sure of it. But you can't take off like that when we are under attack. Do you understand?"

She did, and no matter how much Dominique's words had gotten under her skin, she knew she shouldn't allow herself to be baited into hasty actions that went against the code. "I do."

"It's clear that Dominique didn't abduct you, so she must've been trying to recruit you. Tell me what she offered."

Neal kept her expression neutral. She should've known Siobhan would anticipate Dominique's moves and expect her to share everything she'd learned, and it was only Dominique's voice in her head that caused her to hesitate before responding. "She and Mikhail are taking Mikhail's business mainstream. They're opening speakeasies all over the area, designed to attract well-heeled customers who will pay big bucks for discretion. They're set up for gambling and sex, and I wouldn't be surprised if they sold exclusive memberships. Dominique is going to use the Mancuso name to give the whole enterprise legitimacy."

Siobhan exchanged a look with Royal who nodded in response.

"What?" Neal asked.

"Royal's brother managed to trace the funds Dominique squirreled away after Don Carlo died. She's already started to make transfers to accounts offshore." Siobhan turned to Ana. "I don't suppose you know anything about that?"

Neal caught the accusing tone. "She came to us, remember?"

Ana placed a hand on her leg. "It's all right, Neal." She faced Siobhan. "No, I don't know anything about it, but I can find out. I've spent years tracking Mikhail's movements. If Dominique is sending money to his accounts, I can get you access. Would that be enough to prove that I am not working with him?"

"Possibly." Siobhan closed her eyes for a moment. "Forgive me if I don't know who I can trust anymore, but, Neal, you didn't exactly answer my question. You told me what Dominique is up to, but not what she tempted you with."

This was it. Once she divulged the details, any deal with Dominique was off the table. But had it ever really been a legit offer? Dominique cozying up to her now was a strategy, employed to not only get under Siobhan's skin, but to divide the family in ways that could leave them fractured forever. The question really came down to whether she was a respected member of this family or a servant, rewarded just enough to keep happy but never really partaking of the spoils.

"I'll say it again. You made me a capo in this family. Don't you trust me not to be tempted by someone who doesn't have our best interests at heart?"

"I've trusted you for many years to protect my life and you've always done so with no thought to your own," Siobhan said. "Of course I trust you to be loyal, but knowing what others choose to offer you to switch sides is ammunition we can use against them. I guess the real question here is whether you trust me. Do you?"

Siobhan's stare was fierce and unwavering, and Neal met it for several seconds before looking over at Ana. She didn't need approval, but she wanted affirmation from someone who'd seen her at her most vulnerable. With her sister. Naked in the hotel. She wasn't sure when it had started to matter, but Ana's assessment was important to her, and she breathed a sigh of relief when Ana nodded in response to the unspoken question. "Yes, I do trust you." She cleared her throat and dug in her pocket for the paper Dominique had handed her. "She gave me this."

Siobhan unfolded the paper and scanned its contents. "That's a big role and a lot of money."

"Yes. More than I've ever made before. It should tell you something that I'm sharing this with you."

"It does." Siobhan handed the paper to Royal. "They must expect to make a killing in their new business."

Royal read the paper and gave it back to Neal. "They will." She pointed at the paper. "That's a tiny fraction of what they can hope to make. The demand for black market gambling and prostitution is strong and the booze they'll sell is gravy."

"There's more."

Everyone turned to Ana who hadn't said much up to now. "What?" Neal asked.

Ana shifted in her seat and grimaced. "The prostitutes. He'll have some out front who are like the ones at Francine's." She shared a look with Siobhan. "But he'll have more in the back room that appeal to a more prurient interest."

"Say what you mean," Neal said.

"She means they are young. Too young. Right, Ana?" Siobhan asked. "And, let me guess, they may not be here of their own free will."

Ana clenched her jaw. "I told you he is a monster."

Neal placed an arm around her shoulder and pulled her close. She felt Siobhan's and Royal's eyes on her, but she didn't care, and she couldn't begin to define her feelings. "We have to stop them."

Her words hung in the air, buoyed by honor. Stopping Mikhail wasn't simply good business, it was the right thing to do. If he'd known what was on the horizon and that his daughter was involved, Don Carlo would've sent Michael and a fleet of other Mancuso foot soldiers to take Mikhail out and spirit Dominique away until she regained her senses. But Don Carlo wasn't here, the Dominique she'd talked to yesterday was fully aware of what she was doing, and stopping Mikhail by brute force was likely to start a war rather than remedy the problem. No, they'd have to do things Ana's way if they wanted to solve the problem that was Mikhail, and if they were going to do things her way, then she needed to be part of the plan. The prospect was daunting, but doable. She was a capo now and part of her role was choosing who would work with her. Ana was her first choice and the perfect right hand, and the fact she was also a fantastic lover didn't factor into the equation.

At least that's what she told herself. What other choice did she have?

"And that's why you're the perfect person to help us."

Ana had expected things between her and Neal to change, but she hadn't expected the complete turnaround, and Neal urging Siobhan and Royal to join forces with her was welcome, but surprising still. Sex in a fancy hotel apparently had a transformational effect.

But it hadn't been just sex. Every minute she'd spent with Neal over the past twenty-four hours had revealed more and more interesting revelations about the bodyguard turned capo, and the fact she was a wonderful lover was only one of the most interesting things about her. Seeing Neal with her sister told Ana she had a tender heart, one that she'd guarded carefully, but was now prepared to bare, and Ana took the gesture with the gravitas it deserved. She wouldn't be responsible for breaking that heart, no matter what happened with Mikhail, but she would do everything in her power to make sure he went down.

"Of course, I'll help," she said. "It'll be more difficult for you to gain access to him now that the rift in your family is official, but I can get close to him whenever I want."

She saw the wince on Neal's face, but she had to ignore it if she wanted to get through this. "He's not going to simply fade away. There needs to be a permanent solution."

"How do we know you're not simply trying to get us to kill your husband so you don't have to?" Siobhan asked.

"You don't. But you should know enough about me to know I keep my word. I told you I would help your cash flow and I brought money. I told you Neal had disappeared, and she had. You sent me to find her, and I brought her back to you. I don't know what you require in terms of proof when it comes to loyalty, but I believe I've displayed I have what it takes. Do you disagree?"

Royal spoke first. "We don't. I..." She glanced over at Siobhan who was pretending to act like she wasn't eavesdropping. "We, believe you are sincere when you say you want to break free of Mikhail, but you can understand our caution."

"I do, but the time for patience has ended. It's time for action."

"I should take the deal Dominique offered," Neal said. "Run the club downtown. It's the perfect way to get close to their operation."

Ana's stomach clenched at the idea of Neal in close proximity to Mikhail and Dominique. "They're more dangerous than you realize. This isn't the same as selling bootlegged whiskey."

Neal laughed. "You make it sound like we're playing games over here." Her expression turned serious. "I know what danger is and I'm not scared to face it head-on."

Ana looked at Siobhan and Royal. "It's a bad idea," she implored them. "You have to tell her that."

"I'm not sure it is," Royal said. "It might be brilliant. And it's a perfect way to find out if Dominique was serious about the offer or if she was merely baiting us to see how we would react."

"Royal's right," Neal said. "If she's bluffing, we call it, but if she was serious about giving me a job with total access to their operation, it's the perfect way to lay the groundwork to take them both down."

Ana wanted to scream. Simply hearing the words "Royal's right" come out of Neal's mouth convinced her she didn't appreciate the scope of what she was being asked to do. She wanted to pull Neal aside, talk to her privately, but she sensed Siobhan and Royal would become suspicious—not a good plan when she'd worked hard to gain their trust. She settled on a simple "Let's think about it."

"Ana." Neal spoke her name in a firm but quiet tone that told her the decision had already been made.

"Yes?"

"I have to go now. We've been back for hours, and Dominique is probably watching me, and knows that we're with Siobhan. She has to know that with every hour I don't get back to her, there's a chance I'm plotting against her."

"Which you are."

"Right. For all this plotting to work, there has to be a plan."

"And your plan is to help them. I don't think so." She watched the features on Neal's face freeze, but she couldn't stop the lecture. "This isn't a plan, it's a poorly executed maneuver. Trust me when I tell you that they are several steps ahead of the game and no matter how smart you are, how well you prepare, they will find you out and they will not merely kick you out of their house. You will be finished and there won't be anything I or Royal or Siobhan can do."

"Not true," Siobhan said. "We may be weaker than we were, but we still have friends." She placed a hand on Neal's shoulder. "Trust me when I tell you we will not let anything happen to you," she said before turning to face Ana. "There are others who would benefit from your husband going out of business, and our enemy's enemy is our friend. I can't tell you more, but Neal can vouch for my ability to negotiate deals, even with adversaries. I *earned* the title of consigliere."

Ana studied Siobhan's face, searching for any sign she was being played, but she found none. It all came down to the same thing. She trusted Neal and Neal trusted Siobhan. "I will hold you to your promise. You may think I'm nothing more than a bored housewife, anxious to rid myself of a piggish husband, but I too have abilities if not the title to go with them."

"Then, together we should be able to accomplish whatever we set out to do," Siobhan said, holding out her hand.

Ana flicked a glance at Neal who nodded. Resolved to tying her fate to these women, she gripped Siobhan's hand in both of hers. This alliance was her best hope, and she would see it through.

A few minutes later, she and Neal were standing in the lobby. She touched the collar of Neal's shirt, wishing they were not in public. "When you say you have to go now, do you mean right now?"

"Unfortunately, yes. Dominique's going to know I was here, and if she knows that then she knows I was with you. It may already be too late to convince her I'm willing to switch sides."

"Tell her I wanted to meet with you. That I wanted to betray Mikhail."

Neal looked horrified. "No way. She'll tell him. I will not put you in danger."

Ana held up a hand. "Tell her you agreed to meet with me so you could hear what I had to say and report back to her. She's crafty. She may be in business with Mikhail, but I doubt she trusts him. If she thinks there's a way to take him down so that she has total control, don't you think she'll take it?"

"That's a big risk. If she tells Mikhail, they will come for you."

"Then we'll have to trust Siobhan and Royal when they say they have friends looking out for us all." She noted Neal's frown. "What is it?"

Neal shook her head and reached for Ana's hand. "Nothing. I can handle whatever they throw my way, but the idea of them harming you…I don't even want to go there."

"Neither do I." She reluctantly eased away. "Go. Be fierce, but careful. Contact me when you can."

Her stomach sank as she watched Neal leave. Neal was right—pretending to align with Dominique was the smartest thing she could do, but it was also fraught with risk. As if on cue, her phone buzzed with an incoming text. She pulled it out, hoping it was Neal with words of encouragement, but it was Katia's name on the screen. *Where are you? Mikhail is pissed. Tried to calm him down, but he's convinced you're up to something. Call me.*

Great. Mikhail on a tear didn't bode well for Neal. She looked outside, but Neal was no longer in sight, so she fired off a quick text. *He suspects something. Be careful.*

It wasn't much, but it was something and all she could do right now without raising suspicion. Now she had to get back home and convince Katia and Mikhail her sudden disappearance had nothing to do with any long-term plan.

CHAPTER EIGHTEEN

The club was packed, and if this were a completely different enterprise, Neal would be happy to be in charge, but the girls in the back were underage, the house was cheating at cards, and the watered-down alcohol made for nasty cocktails. Everything about this operation was third rate, but the forbidden nature of the business drew crowds who wanted to be in on the secret. Dominique and Mikhail couldn't be happier. Either that or they were hopped up on the coke that flowed freely in the back rooms. Neal was almost tempted to tip off Royal's former employer as a final solution.

"Take a break," Dominique said, her mouth too close to Neal's ear. "You've been on your feet all night. Don't be afraid to sample the merchandise."

"I'm good. Thanks." Neal tapped one of the waiters on the arm and pointed to a table full of fat old men who were holding up fists full of money. "Take care of them," she told him before turning back to Dominique. "Why don't you take a break? I've got this."

"I will if you will." Dominique pointed to the door behind the bar. "Come hang out with me." She grabbed the lapels of Neal's jacket. "That's an order."

Neal reluctantly followed Dominique to the hidden room where the money was collected and counted as it came in. A big job since there was a lot of it. Dominique pointed to one of the chairs and motioned for her to sit.

"I'm going to make you a drink. It's something special I've been trying out." She slurred her words slightly as she staggered over to a well-stocked bar in the corner. Not a great look for the club owner, but Neal wasn't here to critique Dominique on her professionalism.

"That's great."

She was two sips into the overly sweet concoction when Mikhail barreled into the room in his I'm-the-most-important-person-in-the-world way. She went instantly on edge and started breathing slow deep breaths to remain steady.

"What is she doing in here?" Mikhail bellowed, pointing in her direction. "You know she wants to fuck my wife, right?"

"Is that so?" Dominique asked in a bored voice. "You think everyone wants to fuck your wife. Maybe you should fuck her more to keep her happy enough not to want to stray."

"She only likes women. It's sad for her, but this one," he pointed at her again. "This one is tall enough to be a man, but it's not the same. Right?"

Neal pushed to the edge of her seat, ready to kick his ass, but Dominique merely rolled her eyes.

"She used to play basketball, but then she refused to pay her end of a debt, so a loan shark broke her leg and she had to quit."

Neal fought to keep her expression neutral, but her head was spinning. Siobhan had told her no one in the family besides her and Don Carlo knew the reason she'd quit the team at Tulane, but one of them must've told Dominique.

Ana knew.

She shook away the pesky thought. Ana had known for all of twenty-four hours and she'd spent almost every minute of that time in her presence. No way had Ana had time to cozy up to Dominique with inside information. With no opportunity and no motive, the whole idea was crazy.

What if she's playing you, and Siobhan, and Royal? Taking out Mikhail would leave Dominique in charge of this new enterprise. Or maybe Ana was subbing in for Mikhail as Dominique's new business partner.

Crazy.

No crazier than the consigliere of a powerful family falling for an FBI agent. Or the FBI agent leaving her job in the middle of an undercover operation and living out in the open like no one from the agency would even care. Siobhan and Royal were acting like they were impervious to law enforcement. What was up with that?

A buzzer went off somewhere in the room and Dominique stiffened mid-pour. She shoved the bottle across the bar and barked at the guy counting the money, telling him to go as she pointed to the back door. Neal stood up and whirled around, looking for the source of the sound and Dominique's panic, but before she could process what was happening, the doors to the room flew open and a swarm of federal agents poured into the room. ATF, DEA, and FBI—an alphabet soup of a task force and, judging by the number of agents, this was no last-minute raid. Seconds later, with her face on the floor and her hands zip-tied behind her back, Neal was certain someone close had betrayed her. The only question was who.

❖

Ana paced the living room of her home, anxious to know what was happening with Neal. She'd contemplated simply showing up at Dominique's club, pretending Mikhail had told her about it, but the risk was too great that he would be there. He might not be the smartest person alive, but he had a weird sixth sense when it came to her and other women, like he knew which ones were important to her, and he'd managed to drive them all away. With most of them it had been easy, but none of them were like Neal who was trained to deal with danger. Mikhail's verbal threats would have little effect on her, but the chance he'd resort to violence made her ill and she wasn't going to risk it for the mere chance of seeing Neal. She would hold out for the long game instead.

"There you are." Katia rushed into the room, her face furrowed with concern. "I was so worried about you and Mikhail was distressed."

"Were you?"

"Of course, I was." Katia stood with her hands on her hips. "You've never disappeared like that. I was afraid that woman you met at Sanctuary had lured you into something dangerous."

A chill went up her spine at the mention of Neal, but she feigned ignorance. "What woman?"

"The really tall one with the strange name. Strange for a woman anyway."

There was no use pretending since Katia had been with her both at Sanctuary and the restaurant where she'd met with Neal to discuss terms of an alliance. "Neal? Please, she was interested in me only to get close to Mikhail's business ventures." She tilted her head. "You seem very invested in my personal life."

Katia pouted. "I'm your best friend. It's my job to look out for you."

"And you've always done such a great job." The lie was easier than the confrontation and more effective since Katia beamed at the praise. She decided to reward her with a nugget of knowledge. "I needed a night away." She breathed deeply. "Mikhail has never begrudged me that. Do you?"

Katia looked surprised. "Me? I'm your most loyal friend. I don't begrudge you anything. You know you can trust me, right?"

Her words were the hallmark of someone who can't be trusted, but Ana acted like nothing was wrong. "Absolutely. May I tell you a secret?"

"Of course you can."

"I think Mikhail might be having an affair with Dominique Mancuso." She dropped the bomb and let it reverberate. If Katia's loyalties were with Mikhail instead of her, she'd waste no time telling him what she'd just said. She already knew the answer, but confirmation would make it easier to cut ties with Katia completely, and in the name of their former friendship, it was the least she could do.

"An affair?" Katia laughed. "That's ridiculous."

Ana was genuinely surprised by her reaction. "What? You think he only has eyes for me? Have you met him?"

"He may do things men do, but he always comes home to you."

"'Things men do'? That's a poor excuse for bad behavior. You think that should be enough?"

"When it's a man who works as hard as he does to make a nice life for his family? Absolutely."

Ana wanted to back away from Katia, order her out of the room. Katia's words made her sick. Had they ever really been friends or had there only been the illusion of closeness formed over the years? A convenient connection fostered by her own isolation. There had been a time when she'd trusted Katia with her life, but now she didn't even trust her to make a phone call on her behalf. But not trusting her meant the smartest move she could make was to keep her close. "What are you up to today?"

"Francine's called and said our dresses are ready. I know you're probably not interested in shopping, but I could use a few things."

"I'm interested." Ana injected what she hoped sounded like sincere enthusiasm into her voice. "Let's make a day of it." Shopping was better than sitting around, wondering what was happening with Neal. She reached for the house phone. "I'll have Sergei get the car ready." Best to have Mikhail's man drive her around to document she was up to nothing other than a frivolous shopping spree. She pressed the button to reach Sergei when someone pounded on her door.

She placed a hand over the phone. "What is it?"

"Open the door. Now."

Recognizing Sergei's voice, she motioned to Katia to open the door, and steeled herself for the intrusion. He strode into the room, took the phone from her hand, and spoke into it. "Go into lockdown. Now. No one gets in or out except for Mikhail. Do you understand?"

"What's going on?" Ana asked, her voice shaking. She didn't have to fake the anxiety—something bad had happened and she was about to be stuck in this house, unable to do anything about it and limited to the information Mikhail's men chose to share.

"Nothing that concerns you." He wagged a finger between her and Katia. "Stay put. No one leaves the house."

He turned and walked out of the room without further comment. Ana wanted to yell after him, command him to stay and explain what was happening, but Sergei was loyal only to Mikhail. If she wanted information, she'd have to find another way to get it.

"What's happening?" Katia asked.

"How should I know? I've been sitting right here with you."

Katia frowned. "No need to snap at me."

"I'm sorry." Ana ran through a list of possible scenarios. She needed to be alone to think, but she also had to be careful not to alert Katia she suspected something really big was happening. Had Neal taken out Mikhail? They hadn't even formulated a plan. Perhaps she'd seen a window of opportunity and taken it, plans be damned. She needed to talk to Neal, and she needed to do it now, but Katia showed no signs of leaving her suite. "I didn't mean to bark at you like that. You know how Sergei always rubs me the wrong way. It's probably some misunderstanding." She bit her bottom lip and assumed a serious expression. "You know, he likes you. Maybe you could talk to him. See if he'll tell you what's happening." She injected a slight quiver in her voice. "It would put my mind at ease to know Mikhail is okay."

"I'm not sure you're right, but I suppose I could try and get him to talk to me." Katia placed a hand on hers. "If it would comfort you."

Ana resisted the urge to jerk her hand out of Katia's grasp and endured the charade. "It would be a great comfort," she said, injecting as much innuendo as she could muster into the simple statement.

She waited a full sixty seconds from the time Katia cleared her door before she dug her spare phone out of her bag. Her thumbs hovered over the keyboard while she thought about what to say, but when she considered someone else might be able to read the message, nothing worked. A call would be better. No record of what was said, and she'd know right away from the tone of Neal's voice whether or not she was in trouble. She pressed the buttons on the screen and waited through the rings. One, two, three, four—way past reasonable, but she couldn't make herself hang up. Five, six…

"Who is this?"

Not Neal's voice. A man. An impatient, gruff man. She could choose to speak and try and find out who he was, or she could hang up and hope she'd gotten the wrong number. She glanced at the phone. The number wasn't wrong. She lowered her voice and prayed she'd be able to hide her distinctive accent. "Who is this?"

"Who are you? This number belongs to a felon. Why are you calling her?"

Whoever he was, he was more interested in using scare tactics than coaxing information out of her. She faked a sob. "That's what I was afraid of. Did you catch her before she could do something really bad?"

"Tell me who you are, and I'll tell you more," the voice said.

Not going to happen. She clicked off the line and her brain went on overdrive. Her house was on lockdown, Mikhail was on the run, and a stranger was answering Neal's phone. She needed to get out of here and figure out what was going on, but getting past Sergei was going to be difficult. She looked at the time. Katia was probably still in the process of trying to butter him up. If she left now, there was a slight chance she could make it past Sergei's men.

She opened the secret safe she'd had installed in her dressing table and stuffed her biggest purse with cash. She grabbed her phone, and slipped out of her suite, pausing at the top of the landing. She could hear movement below and several shouts, but it sounded more like panic than action. She edged away from the main staircase, back toward the servants' entrance and ducked into the hallway the household staff used to move through the house without mingling with their higher-ups.

Within a few minutes, she was in the kitchen, threading her way through the massive rows of appliances and cookware more suitable for a banquet hall than a house with less than a dozen occupants, including staff. When she finally reached the back door, she pushed through it, thankful Sergei's men weren't smart enough to think to block this particular exit.

She slipped behind the wheel of one of the BMW sedans the security detail drove. The key was in the ignition, and she wasted no time gunning out of the driveway and onto the road. The drive back to Dallas wasn't quick. I-30 was packed. She kept one hand on the steering wheel and fumbled in her pocket for her phone, the only item she'd managed to bring with her. She punched the numbers for Siobhan, but the person who answered wasn't her.

"It's Ana. Royal, is that you?"

"Yes. Siobhan got called away on an emergency."

"Let me guess. It has something to do with Mikhail."

"It does. The feds raided the club."

"'The feds' sounded funny coming from Royal's mouth, but Ana didn't have time to dwell on the irony of their conversation. "Tell me Neal's okay."

"She was arrested. So was Dominique. Mikhail managed to get out before the raid. I don't suppose you know anything about that?"

Ana was both shocked and hurt at Royal's insinuation she was somehow involved. "You think I told Mikhail that a raid was coming? I suppose you have some theory about why I even knew about it in the first place. And I guess I've been entertaining myself by telling you that I want to get rid of my husband, when I secretly pine for him and would do anything to keep him safe." Her voice rose. "Is that what you think?"

"Look, I know that when you're around there's trouble. Remember the night of the bomb threat at the museum? The night Siobhan spoke about the generous gift her family was donating to the museum. You were there."

Ana laughed as she dodged around a slower car and sped up to regain the time she'd spent following slowly behind. "I've always heard that American police are very paranoid, now I know it's true. You think a few loosely related facts solve the answer to any question, but anything loosely woven is subject to falling apart when you pull at the edges." She jerked the steering wheel to avoid running up on the bumper of the vehicle in front of her. "Now, tell me what I want to know. Is Neal okay? Isn't Siobhan some big shot lawyer? Why hasn't she used her influence to get Neal out?"

"She's working on getting her out, but it's not a simple process. Trust me, Ana, you're better off not knowing more."

Royal's tone only fueled her frustration. "Don't be condescending to me. I'm headed to the courthouse. That's where they would take her, right?"

"Not today. It's after six. They'll hold her until morning at one of the local jails, and then they'll bring her to court for a detention hearing. You should go home and wait to hear from us."

Home. Royal was referring to the palatial mansion she'd just escaped, but she'd never thought of that place as home, only a place to reside until she could escape her life with Mikhail. She couldn't go back there now. Not after the way she'd left, but more importantly, she was done pretending, and if Mikhail showed up, he would instantly suspect her plans to leave him. Better to simply do it now and suffer the consequences. She looked down at her phone, the one she'd purchased without Mikhail's knowledge so he could no longer trace her movements. It was all she had, but at least it was a lifeline. This car, on the other hand, was an anchor. He likely had tracking devices installed on all of their vehicles and the faster she ditched it, the safer she would be.

"I can't go home. I had to slip out and now they'll be looking for me. If Mikhail finds me, he'll never believe I'm still loyal to him. Contact me at this number when you find out what's happening with Neal. If you don't, I will show up at the courthouse and tell the judge everything I know. About all of you."

She hung up before Royal could answer, took a deep breath, and took her foot off the accelerator. Despite the big threat she'd just made, now was not the time to trade haste for security. She needed a plan, and she needed a quiet place to think it through because she was dead set now on not only escaping her current life, but finding a way for Neal to be part of her future.

CHAPTER NINETEEN

Neal had been at the federal courthouse in downtown Dallas more times than she could count, but only ever in her role as Siobhan's bodyguard. Most of the time, she dropped Siobhan off at the front door, parked the car, and waited outside, relying on the security inside to protect her boss, but sometimes, when the case was particularly charged, she accompanied Siobhan inside, making herself as unobtrusive as possible while remaining vigilant against any potential threats.

Today was completely different. Instead of rolling up to the building in the Range Rover, she'd been transported there in the back of a windowless van. She hadn't walked into the courthouse of her own free will, instead she'd been led by a team of federal marshals, and her progress was impaired by chain that linked her ankles and the handcuffs on her wrists. Now she was sitting on a hard bench in a holding cell, somewhere in the building, wondering what would happen next.

As the moments ticked by, questions flooded her mind. She'd seen Dominique arrested as well. Where was she being held? Who had tipped off the cops? Common sense told her it could've been anyone, but reality dictated it would need to be someone with something big to gain. The niggling doubts she'd had about Ana at the club last night inched back into her head, gnawing their way through her feelings. Had she let her attraction to Ana cloud her judgment? She didn't want to believe it, but the fact Mikhail had gotten away was a sure indicator he'd been tipped off.

But Ana's insistence that Mikhail was a monster she couldn't bear to be around had always rung true. She was one hundred percent right about the monster part, and Neal couldn't imagine the woman she'd gotten to know would want to be tethered to someone like Mikhail. Could she have been so wrong?

No, there was no way that Ana would've protected Mikhail, but she might've tipped off the feds about the club to get him arrested and out of her life. Not a permanent solution, but it could buy her time to find her own way out.

Too many possibilities and too little sleep. Neal put her head in her hands and pushed away the jumbled mess of thoughts. All she knew for sure right now was that she was in big trouble, and she didn't know how she was going to get out of it. Any other made member of the family could expect the consigliere to show up and save the day, but it wasn't that simple now. She might be made, but if Ana was the source of this takedown, it was a problem of her own making, and the family would likely not intervene. Besides, Siobhan was no longer the consigliere with time to solve the problems of family members who'd gotten themselves arrested. More likely, a public defender with no clue about the intricacies of this situation would show up and go through the rote steps of a detention hearing. She'd be held over for trial, shipped back to the county jail to rot until her next court date.

A loud buzz at the door interrupted her thoughts and she looked up to see one of the marshals standing in the doorway. "Stand up," he barked.

She wanted to tell him to shove it, but her bravado wouldn't get her very far when she didn't have a fancy private lawyer to back it up, so instead she pushed off the bench and stood in the middle of the room with her arms stretched out. He unlocked the door and walked in, then patted her down again. She wasn't sure what he expected to find since she'd been sitting in the empty cell since she'd gotten here, but she didn't protest. When he finally finished, he cuffed her hands and led her out of the cell. They walked past a few other empty cells to a door down the hall. He knocked on the door and a familiar female voice called out, "Come in."

Siobhan was seated at the head of a table in what looked to be a conference room. The marshal motioned for her to take a seat a few feet away from Siobhan who placed a finger on her lips, signaling for her to keep quiet while he was still in the room. Fine by her since she didn't really know what to say.

"Take off her cuffs," Siobhan said. "I'm going to need her to sign some papers."

He grimaced but did as she ordered. She rubbed her wrists while Siobhan told him to leave the room.

"Are you okay?" she asked once the door closed behind him.

"Yes, but I'd prefer not to have to go back to that jail if there's anything you can do about that."

"I can absolutely do something about that, but first tell me everything that happened last night from when you showed up at the club to the moment the feds raided the place."

Neal recounted the evening and included every detail. The drugs, the girls, the stacks of cash. "Dominique was arrested at the same time I was, but Mikhail got away." She hung her head. "I'm worried that Ana may have tipped him off."

Siobhan cocked her head. "What makes you think that?"

"I don't want to believe it's true, but I think he knew about the raid."

"Maybe he's simply lucky. Do you really believe this woman you've grown fond of would do such a thing?"

"I don't, but we've been on opposite sides since the start."

"I know a bit about that."

Neal managed a smile. "I guess you do." She wanted to ask how and when Siobhan had been sure she could trust Royal, but she feared the question might be insulting. "She might not have tipped off Mikhail, but she could've tipped off the feds about the club as a way to get him out of the picture."

"I suppose that's true, but Ana strikes me as the type of woman who would favor a more direct hit on her enemy." Siobhan leaned forward. "Besides, I know who contacted the feds about the club and it wasn't Ana." A few beats of silence built up the suspense before she announced, "It was Royal."

As if on cue, Royal stepped into the room, followed by a man in a suit, Neal didn't recognize. They took a seat at the table across from her.

"This is Special Agent in Charge Mark Wharton. My boss," Royal said.

Neal turned to Siobhan. "What the hell is going on here?"

Siobhan gave her a stern look. "Take a breath, Neal, and listen to what we have to say." She cleared her throat.

"Mr. Wharton is investigating both Dominique Mancuso and Mikhail Petrov. In my capacity as attorney for you, I have prepared a dossier of information for him, detailing their illegal activities, but he would like to hear directly from you." She reached into her briefcase and pulled out two stacks of papers and pushed them toward her.

"That first set of documents is the dossier, and the second is the offer Mr. Wharton has prepared. In exchange for your truthful testimony, he's prepared to offer you complete immunity and protection. We'll go over the offer in private, but I wanted Mr. Wharton to come in here and tell you himself that he will stand behind his promises. Mr. Wharton?"

Neal recognized the steel in Siobhan's tone from the times she'd seen her in court and at Don Carlo's side, dealing with adversaries. Siobhan was signaling to her to be quiet and leave things to her, and while she chafed at the inability to control her own destiny, she knew better than to disobey.

"That's correct," Wharton said. "I understand you have valuable information and we're willing to discuss a mutually beneficial arrangement." He pointed at the papers on the table. "I'll give you a few minutes to discuss those with Ms. Collins." He stood and looked at his watch. "The judge will be on the bench in twenty minutes."

Siobhan waited until he'd left the room and been gone for several seconds before speaking. "Questions?"

Neal looked from her to Royal and back again. "Too many." She lifted the offer letter from the table. "You want me to cooperate with the feds?"

"I do."

"She's changed you." She jerked her head in Royal's direction. "What would Don Carlo say about this?"

"My father would admire my ability to be resilient in the face of destruction, but it's not your place to question my loyalty."

Neal hung her head. "I'm sorry. You're right. But I'm having a hard time understanding what's happening right now."

"I'll explain, but I need you to listen carefully." Siobhan pointed toward the door and motioned from her ear to her mouth to indicate someone might be listening. Neal knew she was indicating she would need to speak in code. "Do you understand?"

"I do."

"Good. Royal Scott is an FBI agent, and she infiltrated the Mancuso family to see if they had ties to Mikhail Petrov."

Neal started to make some crack about how of course Royal was an agent, but then it struck her that whoever was listening in might not know she knew. "What? No way." She hoped her pretend surprise sounded sincere.

"Yes, it's true. She came to me with a plan and I've been helping her implement it in order to ferret out who in the family would do such a thing."

"It's Dominque." Neal said.

Siobhan raised her eyebrows at her off script interjection. "We suspect it is her, yes."

"I can prove it." Neal reached for her pocket before she remembered all her belongings had been taken from her when she was arrested. "I have photos. Taken at the new club where she's in business with Mikhail."

Siobhan shot a look at Royal who stood and walked out of the room. When she was gone, Siobhan leaned close to her. "Do you really?"

"I do."

"Taking those was a big risk."

"I'm not accustomed to taking small ones."

"True." Siobhan tapped the papers in front of her. "Do you want to know what you're being offered?"

"Do you really think I'm going to take any deal the government is offering?"

"I know you will. They are offering to place you in the witness protection program in exchange for your testimony about Dominique and Mikhail."

Neal took a moment to absorb the words. Witness protection was for snitches and rats who didn't have the courage to stand behind their convictions. That wasn't her and she said so.

"Neal, Royal and I have been cooperating with the FBI as part of a deal we've worked out. That deal includes you." She jabbed at the papers. "You've spent years protecting me and it's my turn to return the favor."

"It was never a favor and you know it."

"You're right. It was an obligation, but you fulfilled it with honor. Did you honestly think you would be held to it for the rest of your life?"

She hadn't ever considered the debt would be repaid. Not as long as Sarah was alive. Siobhan paid her well, but she'd never be able to afford the level of care she received on her salary alone. Becoming made would mean she'd be able to earn more, but it didn't break the bonds of duty. Now Siobhan was offering her a way out, but what would that mean for Sarah? "I can't go into hiding. I have commitments besides you."

Siobhan nodded. "I know. I promise she will receive state-of-the-art care wherever you wind up."

Neal didn't bother arguing the point since she knew Siobhan would make it so, but the promise didn't negate her dilemma entirely. "There's someone else."

Siobhan studied her for a moment until it finally struck her who she was talking about. She shook her head vigorously. "No. That's out of the question."

"You just finished telling me she wasn't involved."

"He will spend his days looking for her. Both your lives will be in danger."

"Are you telling me you do not recommend aligning with people who appear to be your enemies? Because I don't think you're in a position to give out that kind of advice."

"Touché." Siobhan's expression was pained. "I want to give you this, but I've expended all the leverage we have to buy freedom for you, me, and Royal. They'll even let you choose where you want to go, as long as it's not Texas or Louisiana. I don't have anything left to trade. And they aren't going to expend a spot in the program for a Russian citizen unless she has state secrets."

Neal knew what Siobhan was saying was true, but the idea of never seeing Ana again left her cold. "I won't go."

"You have to go. Sarah won't be safe if you don't."

Shit. Siobhan was right, of course, but that didn't make her feel any better about it. The truth was she was going from one form of servitude to another, and she'd never be free. "Give me a piece of paper."

"What?"

Neal jabbed a finger at Siobhan's briefcase. "Paper. I want to write a note and you're going to deliver it for me."

Siobhan handed her a pen and a pad, and she started writing. She had so much she wanted to say, but she curtailed the impulse to fill the page with sentiment and focused the most direct, yet covert, message to convey her desire. As Royal reentered the room, she skimmed what she'd written. She could write more, but the gist was there and if she kept going, she might change her mind. She set the pen down, folded the note, and handed it to Siobhan. "You'll make sure she gets this?"

"I will."

Neal had to trust her. She might never see Ana again, but she would be damned if she didn't let her know how she'd made her feel in the short time they'd been together. "Where do I sign?"

CHAPTER TWENTY

Ana stood in front of Siobhan's door and smacked it with her fist. She'd been pressing the doorbell for several minutes with no response, and her frustration was deep. She raised her fist to bang on the door again when she heard a voice over her shoulder.

"No one's home."

She whirled to see Siobhan and Royal standing behind her. "Where is she?"

"Come inside," Siobhan said, moving past her to put her key in the lock.

"No. You can answer my questions out here. Where is she?" Royal grabbed her arm, but she dug in her heels. "No."

Siobhan waved Royal off. "I have something for you, but you have to come inside to get it. It's from her."

Ana sighed in resignation. It had been a week since the raid at the club. No one had heard from Mikhail, and when she tried to find Neal in the system it was like she'd vanished. Dominique was in federal custody and the only people who might have an idea of what had happened to Neal were standing in front of her. She was out of choices, and she knew it, so she followed them into the apartment.

"I didn't want to come here, but you haven't responded to my calls," she said.

"Sit down," Siobhan said. "Let's talk."

She followed Siobhan's lead and settled onto the couch. She took a moment to catch her breath and glanced around to see the apartment was looking bare except for stacks of boxes lining the walls. "Are you moving?"

"Yes."

"Into the Mancuso mansion?"

Siobhan's expressed was pained. "No." She reached for Royal's hand. "We have other plans."

Ana winced with her own pain. She'd had plans too until Neal disappeared off the face of the earth. Now she was hiding out from Mikhail instead of taking over his business, an avenue of escape now completely cut off from her since Mikhail's men believed she'd betrayed him. She'd learned that her father had recalled Katia back to Russia, probably to grill her about what had been happening here, and once he learned of what he would deem her indiscretions, that home would be foreclosed to her as well. She'd spent a lifetime plotting her freedom, but she hadn't expected it in such a dramatic package. At this point, she didn't care about ruling an empire. All she wanted was the simple pleasures of a small, quiet house where she could live out her days with someone she loved, but even that wasn't possible. Neal was gone, she was on the run, and there was no one she could turn to except the women seated with her now and they were on the way out. "You're leaving."

"Yes. We're starting over. Somewhere new."

"Where are you going?"

"Do you really want to know?" Siobhan asked. "Think carefully before you respond. Knowledge can make you a target."

"Never mind," Ana said, not bothering to hide her despair. "It doesn't matter anyway."

"Wait here."

Siobhan stood abruptly and walked out of the room. Ana faced Royal, but when she saw pity reflected back at her, she looked away. She didn't need pity, but she did need answers. When Siobhan returned, she was going to get some.

"This is for you," Siobhan said as she walked back into the room. She handed over a folded piece of paper. "She made me promise to give it to you. I planned to find you before we left."

Ana held it up but didn't open it. "This is it? Where is she?"

"She's gone. She didn't have a choice."

"Everyone has a choice."

"It's a nice sentiment, but not entirely true," Siobhan said. "I would have lived my life differently had I known Don Carlo was my father, but since I didn't know, I didn't have a choice. You could have chosen not to marry Mikhail, but I expect you didn't have other palatable options. Yes, we have choices, but circumstances often curtail the best ones, leaving us with no way out. Neal is gone and you should go too because if he finds you, he will kill you."

She knew what Siobhan said was true, but she felt so lost and she couldn't stop the feeling that if she could talk to Neal, she might be able to find peace. She looked at the paper in her hand. It wasn't the same as talking to Neal, but perhaps reading her words might give her some form of closure, if not satisfaction. "I should go," she said, not wanting to be alone again, but also not wanting to read Neal's note until she was alone.

She walked a block and hailed a cab from a hotel nearby to take her across town to the room she'd rented for the week. It was dingy and dusty, and she hated it, but she'd told herself it was temporary, until she could find Neal and plan a future with her. Looking back, she'd been silly to think what they'd had was anything other than the attraction that comes from being thrown together by circumstance. It wasn't lasting, it wasn't true. Neal had left without a real good-bye, and she was left with nothing more than the note on the table in front of her.

Read it.

What was the point?

Read it.

Tired of battling the voice, she picked up the paper, skimmed it at first, and then settled in to study every word. She read it three times, each time taking a break in between to pace the small room. She scoured the words one more time before folding the paper back up and hiding it with the cash she'd managed to squirrel away before she'd gone on the run.

Yes, Neal was gone, and she wasn't coming back, but that didn't mean she had to sit around in this dump and whine about it. She was Anastasia Petrov and she had choices to make.

❖

"Same table?"

"Yes, please." Neal slipped a twenty into the host's hand as he led her to the table that gave her the best view of the front of the room. The same waiter who'd served her the past seven days approached with a smile.

"Good afternoon, ma'am."

"Luke, when are you going to stop calling me that?" Neal grinned to soften the remark. "Seriously, I've been called a lot of things, but ma'am is the absolute worst." She held out her hand. "It's Darby. Darby Lassiter." Her tongue tripped over her new name. Everything she'd read about witness protection said most people got to keep their first name, but her handler had made her change hers. Too distinctive, he said. She'd shrugged it off at the time and chosen a name that symbolized her newfound freedom, but she'd hardly used it at all since she'd arrived in New York City. It was time to try out her new self.

Except there was nothing new about her. She was the same person she'd been in Dallas, but jobless and alone except for the sister who didn't even know she was there. She'd had no contact with Siobhan other than a package that had arrived the day before, full of cash and a typed note that told her to be patient, love would find her. It wasn't like Siobhan to be so sentimental, but falling for Royal had changed her, softened her around the edges. Neal used to think that was a bad thing, but who was she to judge? If Siobhan was happy, then how she chose to move through life was entirely up to her.

But Siobhan had been wrong about love finding her. She'd come to this hotel for the last seven days, checked in for her reservation in the restaurant and taken high tea with women in furs, laden with shopping bags. They all sat in groups, giggling, gossiping, and gorging on three-tiered treats and glass after glass of champagne as if these indulgences were the only important things in the world. She didn't belong here, and she didn't belong with a woman who would want to be in this place. But day after day, she returned, hoping against hope Ana Petrov would walk through those doors and join her for tea. And whatever else life might hold.

"The usual?"

She looked up and took a moment to focus. She had to stop drifting off like that. She might be in witness protection, but she could still be in danger if she wasn't careful. "Sorry. Yes, the Prince of Wales, please." She'd felt silly at first, ordering high tea, but she'd come to love the assortment of sweets and savories. When she finally gave up on Ana, she'd have to find another spot to indulge her new habit since at a hundred bucks a pop, her money wasn't going to last long here.

"I'll be right back with your tea, ma'—sorry, Ms. Lassiter."

She smiled at him as he started to walk away, but her smile froze when she spotted a woman grab his arm. She sprang out of her chair and started toward them, but the woman turned toward her and held up a hand to signal she should stop, and when she saw who it was she instantly obeyed.

"Luke, right?" Ana said.

"Yes, ma'am."

"He calls everyone that," Neal said. "Don't take it personally."

Ana smiled at her. "I kind of like it."

"Duly noted." Neal dropped her voice to a whisper. "You came."

"I did. And I have things to say, but first I need to take care of something." She turned back to Luke. "Change our order to the Tsar Nicholas II. We have many things to discuss, and we'll be needing lots of champagne. Understood?"

"Yes, ma'am." He scurried away as soon as she released him.

Neal took the opportunity to step closer. "You got my note."

"I did." Ana looked up and recited the words. "'If only we'd had a chance to have tea at the Baccarat like you wanted.'"

"And that was enough to tell you where to find me?"

"It was the only clue I had."

Neal led her back to the table, and once they were seated, she dove into the topic at the top of her mind. "We never talked about what would happen when you were free of Mikhail." Her gut churned while she waited for Ana's response.

"No, we didn't." Ana reached her hand across the table and threaded her fingers through Neal's. "Did we need to?"

"I don't." She gripped Ana's hand tighter. "I'm kind of a mess right now. Getting Sarah settled, and I don't have a job, and I live in a tiny apartment, but I feel like I have a chance to start over, to find out who I am and who I can become. Does that make sense?"

"It does. I confess I feel the same. The question becomes is this a journey you want to take on your own or would you like some company?"

Neal stared into her eyes. She knew exactly what she wanted, and for the very first time in her life the choice wasn't about duty or debt, but only about what she wanted. And she only wanted one thing.

"I want to build a new life with you. Please tell me that's what you want too."

Tears formed in Ana's eyes, but the big smile signaled she was crying tears of happiness as she answered in the very best way. "You're all I ever wanted. I love you, Neal, and I want to find happiness by your side."

THE END

About the Author

Carsen Taite's goal as an author is to spin tales with plot lines as interesting as the cases she encountered in her career as a criminal defense lawyer. She is the award-winning author of over two dozen novels of romance and romantic intrigue, including the Luca Bennett Bounty Hunter series, the Lone Star Law series, the Legal Affairs romances, and the Courting Danger series.

Books Available from Bold Strokes Books

Lucky in Lace by Melissa Brayden. Straitlaced stationery store owner Juliette Jennings's predictable life unravels when a sexy lingerie shop and its alluring owner move in next door. (978-1-63679-434-1)

Made for Her by Carsen Taite. Neal Walsh is a newly made member of the Mancuso crime family, but will her undeniable attraction to Anastasia Petrov, the wife of her boss's sworn enemy, be the ultimate test of her loyalty? (978-1-63679-265-1)

Off the Menu by Alaina Erdell. Reality TV sensation *Restaurant Redo* and its gorgeous host Erin Rasmussen will arrive to film in chef Taylor Mobley's kitchen. As the cameras roll, will they make the jump from enemies to lovers? (978-1-63679-295-8)

Pack of Her Own by Elena Abbott. When things heat up in a small town, steamy secrets are revealed between Alpha werewolf Wren Carne and her human mate, Natalie Donovan. (978-1-63679-370-2)

Return to McCall by Patricia Evans. Lily isn't looking for romance—not until she meets Alex, the gorgeous Cuban dance instructor at La Haven, a newly opened lesbian retreat. (978-1-63679-386-3)

So It Went Like This by C. Spencer. A candid and deeply personal exploration of fate, chosen family, and the vulnerability intrinsic in life's uncertainties. (978-1-63555-971-2)

Stolen Kiss by Spencer Greene. Anna and Louise share a stolen kiss, only to discover that Louise is dating Anna's brother. Surely, one kiss can't change everything...Can it? (978-1-63679-364-1)

The Fall Line by Kelly Wacker. When Jordan Burroughs arrives in the Deep South to paint a local endangered aquatic flower, she doesn't expect to become friends with a mischievous gin-drinking ghost who complicates her budding romance and leads her to an awful discovery and danger. (978-1-63679-205-7)

To Meet Again by Kadyan. When the stark reality of WW II separates cabaret singer Evelyn and Australian doctor Joan in Singapore, they must overcome all odds to find one another again. (978-1-63679-398-6)

Before She Was Mine by Emma L McGeown. When Dani and Lucy are thrust together to sort out their children's playground squabble, sparks fly leaving both of them willing to risk it all for each other. 978-1-63679-315-3)

Chasing Cypress by Ana Hartnett Reichardt. Maggie Hyde wants to find a partner to settle down with and help her run the family farm, but instead she ends up chasing Cypress. Olivia Cypress. 978-1-63679-323-8)

Dark Truths by Sandra Barret. When Jade's ex-girlfriend and vampire maker barges back into her life, can Jade satisfy her ex's demands, keep Beth safe, and keep everyone's secrets... secret? 978-1-63679-369-6)

Desires Unleashed by Renee Roman. Kell Murphy and Taylor Simpson didn't go looking for love, but as they explore their desires unleashed, their hearts lead them on an unexpected journey. 978-1-63679-327-6)

Maybe, Probably by Amanda Radley. Set against the backdrop of a viral pandemic, Gina and Eleanor are about to discover that loving another person is complicated when you're desperately searching for yourself. 978-1-63679-284-2)

The One by C.A. Popovich. Jody Acosta doesn't know what makes her more furious, that the wealthy Bergeron family refuses to be held accountable for her father's wrongful death, or that she can't ignore her knee-weakening attraction to Nicole Bergeron. 978-1-63679-318-4)

The Speed of Slow Changes by Sander Santiago. As Al and Lucas navigate the ups and downs of their polyamorous relationship, only one thing is certain: romance has never been so crowded. 978-1-63679-329-0)

Tides of Love by Kimberly Cooper Griffin. Falling in love is the last thing on either of their minds, but when Mikayla and Gem meet, sparks of possibility begin to shine, revealing a future neither expected. 978-1-63679-319-1)

Catch by Kris Bryant. Convincing the wife of the star quarterback to walk away from her family was never in offensive coordinator Sutton McCoy's game plan. But standing on the sidelines when a second chance at true love comes her way proves all but impossible. (978-1-63679-276-7)

Hearts in the Wind by MJ Williamz. Beth and Evelyn seem destined to remain mortal enemies but are about to discover that in matters of the heart, sometimes you must cast your fortunes to the wind. (978-1-63679-288-0)

Hero Complex by Jesse J. Thoma. Bronte, Athena, and their unlikely friends must work together to defeat Bronte's arch nemesis. The fate of love, humanity, and the world might depend on it. No pressure. (978-1-63679-280-4)

Hotel Fantasy by Piper Jordan. Molly Taylor has a fantasy in mind that only Lexi can fulfill. However, convincing her to participate could prove challenging. (978-1-63679-207-1)

Last New Beginning by Krystina Rivers. Can commercial broker Skye Kohl and contractor Bailey Kaczmarek overcome their pride and work together while the tension between them boils over into a love that could soothe both of their hearts? (978-1-63679-261-3)

Love and Lattes by Karis Walsh. Cat café owner Bonnie and wedding planner Taryn join forces to get rescue cats into forever homes—discovering their own forever along the way. (978-1-63679-290-3)

Repatriate by Jaime Maddox. Ally Hamilton's new job as a home health aide takes an unexpected twist when she discovers a fortune in stolen artwork and must repatriate the masterpieces and avoid the wrath of the violent man who stole them. (978-1-63679-303-0)

The Hues of Me and You by Morgan Lee Miller. Arlette Adair and Brooke Dawson almost fell in love in college. Years later, they unexpectedly run into each other and come face-to-face with their unresolved past. (978-1-63679-229-3)

A Haven for the Wanderer by Jenny Frame. When Griffin Harris comes to Rosebrook village, the love she finds with Bronte de Lacey creates safe haven and she finally finds her place in the world. But will she run again when their love is tested? (978-1-63679-291-0)

A Spark in the Air by Dena Blake. Internet executive Crystal Tucker is sure Wi-Fi could really help small-town residents, even if it means putting an internet café out of business, but her instant attraction to the owner's daughter, Janie Elliott, makes moving ahead with her plans complicated. (978-1-63679-293-4)

Between Takes by CJ Birch. Simone Lavoie is convinced her new job as an intimacy coordinator will give her a fresh perspective. Instead, problems on set and her growing attraction to actress Evelyn Harper only add to her worries. (978-1-63679-309-2)

Camp Lost and Found by Georgia Beers. Nobody knows better than Cassidy and Frankie that life doesn't always give you what you want. But sometimes, if you're lucky, life gives you exactly what you need. (978-1-63679-263-7)

Felix Navidad by 'Nathan Burgoine. After the wedding of a good friend, instead of Felix's Hawaii Christmas treat to himself, ice rain strands him in Ontario with fellow wedding-guest—and handsome ex of said friend—Kevin in a small cabin for the holiday Felix definitely didn't plan on. (978-1-63679-411-2)

Fire, Water, and Rock by Alaina Erdell. As Jess and Clare reveal more about themselves, and their hot summer fling tips over into true love, they must confront their pasts before they can contemplate a future together. (978-1-63679-274-3)

Lines of Love by Brey Willows. When even the Muse of Love doesn't believe in forever, we're all in trouble. (978-1-63555-458-8)

Manny Porter and The Yuletide Murder by D.C. Robeline. Manny only has the holiday season to discover who killed prominent research scientist Phillip Nikolaidis before the judicial system condemns an innocent man to lethal injection. (978-1-63679-313-9)

Only This Summer by Radclyffe. A fling with Lily promises to be exactly what Chase is looking for—short-term, hot as a forest fire, and one Chase can extinguish whenever she wants. After all, it's only one summer. (978-1-63679-390-0)

Picture-Perfect Christmas by Charlotte Greene. Two former rivals compete to capture the essence of their small mountain town at Christmas, all the while fighting old and new feelings. (978-1-63679-311-5)

Playing Love's Refrain by Lesley Davis. Drew Dawes had shied away from the world of music until Wren Banderas gave her a reason to play their love's refrain. (978-1-63679-286-6)

Profile by Jackie D. The scales of justice are weighted against FBI agents Cassidy Wolf and Alex Derby. Loyalty and love may be the only advantage they have. (978-1-63679-282-8)

Almost Perfect by Tagan Shepard. A shared love of queer TV brings Olivia and Riley together, but can they keep their real-life love as picture perfect as their on-screen counterparts? (978-1-63679-322-1)

Corpus Calvin by David Swatling. Cloverkist Inn may be haunted, but a ghost materializes from Jason Dekker's past and Calvin's canine instinct kicks in to protect a young boy from mortal danger. (978-1-62639-428-5)

Craving Cassie by Skye Rowan. Siobhan Carney and Cassie Townsend share an instant attraction, but are they brave enough to give up everything they have ever known to be together? (978-1-63679-062-6)

Drifting by Lyn Hemphill. When Tess jumps into the ocean after Jet, she thinks she's saving her life. Of course, she can't possibly know Jet is actually a mermaid desperate to fix her mistake before she causes her clan's demise. (978-1-63679-242-2)

Enigma by Suzie Clarke. Polly has taken an oath to protect and serve her country, but when the spy she's tasked with hunting becomes the love of her life, will she be the one to betray her country? (978-1-63555-999-6)

Finding Fault by Annie McDonald. Can environmental activist Dr. Evie O'Halloran and government investigator Merritt Shepherd set aside their conflicting ideas about saving the planet and risk their hearts enough to save their love? (978-1-63679-257-6)

Hot Keys by R.E. Ward. In 1920s New York City, Betty May Dewitt and her best friend, Jack Norval, are determined to make their Tin Pan Alley dreams come true and discover they will have to fight—not only for their hearts and dreams, but for their lives. (978-1-63679-259-0)

Securing Ava by Anne Shade. Private investigator Paige Richards takes a case to locate and bring back runaway heiress Ava Prescott. But ignoring her attraction may prove impossible when their hearts and lives are at stake. (978-1-63679-297-2)

The Amaranthine Law by Gun Brooke. Tristan Kelly is being hunted for who she is and her incomprehensible past, and despite her overwhelming feelings for Olivia Bryce, she has to reject her to keep her safe. (978-1-63679-235-4)

The Forever Factor by Melissa Brayden. When Bethany and Reid confront their past, they give new meaning to letting go, forgiveness, and a future worth fighting for. (978-1-63679-357-3)

The Frenemy Zone by Yolanda Wallace. Ollie Smith-Nakamura thinks relocating from San Francisco to her dad's rural hometown is the worst idea in the world, but after she meets her new classmate Ariel Hall, she might have a change of heart. (978-1-63679-249-1)